DEATH ON THE TOWER

A HIGGINS & HAWKE MYSTERY

LEE STRAUSS

Death on the Tower

Cover by Steven Novak

Cover Illustration by Amanda Sorenson

ISBN: 978-1774090152

1

From the back seat of the taxi, Samantha Hawke leaned close to the driver's ear. "Mister, can't you make this thing go any faster?"

"Goin' as fast I can, lady."

Frustration built up in her chest, and to her dismay she felt sweat build up under the arms of her two-piece, summer dress suit. She removed her straw hat and fanned herself, furious that, not only was she burning up in this slow-moving oven on wheels, but that Johnny Milwaukee would arrive at the scene of the crime before she did. And she'd gotten the tip first!

The nerve of that man, refusing to let her ride along with him in his fancy roadster. He'd get the lead story again. How was she going to prove to her boss she was as good a reporter as the guys if she had to depend on transit and they drove their own cars?

"Finally!" she muttered under her breath as the taxi approached the west side of the Custom House on India Street. She pushed damp locks of honey-blond hair off her face and replaced her hat. She paid the cabbie, then stepped out onto the street with her messenger bag and Kodak box camera strapped over her shoulder.

Her status with the newspaper didn't prevent a wave of scowling to follow her, even as the pedestrians stepped aside. She could see the top of Johnny's messy flop of hair with his fedora tilted jauntily to the side—slightly rebellious like the man on whose head it rested. Max Owen, slender in build and quiet by nature, was with him, snapping photographs with a modern Ensign Cameo camera. Samantha envied the slender, rectangular, leather-encased wood box that when opened, produced a lens contraption on an accordion sleeve. The quality of the lens was notches above her box camera and had a classier focusing ability.

He and Johnny were a professional team and watching them made Samantha feel entirely inadequate.

Which wasn't true. She'd broken the last hot case they'd covered, hadn't she? She couldn't let the surrounding men intimidate her, especially the somewhat handsome and very arrogant Johnny Milwaukee.

He smiled when he saw her.

"Hey, doll. You made it."

"No thanks to you!"

The crowd was extremely large, larger than what constituted an average number of rubbernecks, and Samantha was pushed up against Johnny's back.

She shouted to the hapless offender behind her. "Hey!" To Johnny she added, "What's going on? Why are there so many people on the streets?"

Johnny tilted his head and stared down at Samantha in that superior way that drove her nuts. She bit her tongue at the snide remark bubbling up at the back of her throat. Her patience was rewarded.

"Fire alarm was pulled at the Custom house," Johnny said. "The siren was turned off a minute ago, just before you *finally* got here." This last sentence was delivered with a cocky smile. *He* was the reason she was late. When he looked away, she stabbed him with her elbow.

"Ow!"

Samantha masterfully delivered her faux apology. "Oh, sorry. The crowds..."

She couldn't see the body, a jumper who, according to her contact, had fallen from the seventh floor, on the west side of the Custom House Tower. Police had the area roped off, holding back Custom House employees, the curious, and reporters alike. The *Boston Daily Record* wasn't the only paper on the beat.

Samantha spotted the burly Detective Cluney shouting orders to his underlings—one of whom was Officer Tom Bell. Officer Bell was her contact at the station, a relatively new arrangement, and she tried to catch his eye. Maybe she could tell something by the look on his face, or at the very least, she could indicate her gratitude with a nod of the head, but he didn't turn around.

"It's bad, sweetheart," Johnny said.

Samantha stretched up onto her tiptoes, but still couldn't see through the taller bodies standing in front of her. Johnny had the advantage of height, along with the fact he was male, single, and socially savvy. She'd hate him if he weren't so charming and, admittedly, useful.

"Do you want to climb up onto my back?"

"Very funny, Johnny!" Even if Samantha would risk her dignity to do such a thing in public, her formfitting calf-length dress wouldn't allow for it.

"At least tell me what you see?"

"A splat."

"A splat?"

"Yeah, a splat."

Samantha huffed. Johnny had a habit of being vague when he wanted to.

"Male or female."

"I'm guessing female. 'Cuz of the skirt."

The crowed opened, making way for the city's assistant chief medical examiner, and Samantha's new friend. She called to her, "Haley! Uh, Dr. Higgins!"

Haley turned at Samantha's voice and paused, which gave Samantha a chance to step in before the crowd closed behind them.

"Hello, Samantha," Haley said. "Word travels fast."

"I'm actually surprised I arrived before you did. My taxi was slower than an ox."

"And I'm usually late to the scene," Haley said, blowing loose, wild, dark curls out of her eyes. "As I don't get called until after the police have arrived to assess the damage."

"Does Dr. Guthrie always send you?" Samantha asked.

Haley snorted softly. "Dr. Guthrie prefers to stay at the morgue to drink tea and work on crossword puzzles."

They reached the crime scene rope and the police lifted it for Haley.

The officer dropped it before Samantha could pass. "Sorry, ma'am, police only beyond this point."

Samantha shrugged. She didn't expect to be let in, she only wanted to get closer. And now she had.

She gaped at the gruesome scene before her. The body was a *splat*.

Bile crept up the back of her throat and her

stomach contents surged. Despite the June heat, she felt cold and clammy.

Oh no, was she about to vomit? No! She would never live that down. Johnny would see to that. She closed her eyes, braced herself against her knees, and forced herself to breathe deeply.

"You okay, doll?"

Drat! Johnny Milwaukee was the type of guy who was never there when you needed him and always there when you didn't!

She spat out, "I'm fine."

"Are you sure? You don't look too good"

Samantha straightened, smoothed out her dress, and adjusted the straps of her messenger bag and camera.

"I'm fine. Where's your lackey?" Samantha searched for Max and saw him staring quietly. Embarrassment flickered behind his eyes, and she knew he'd heard her.

"I'm sorry, Max. I didn't mean that. I'm just angry at Johnny and, well, I'm sorry."

A slight smile formed on Max's face, and Samantha knew the mild-mannered man had forgiven her.

Jostling about in crowds was a normal occurrence at crime scenes, so Samantha hadn't expected politeness when it came to a round of pushing and shoving, but she was pleasantly surprised when she looked at the owner of the English-accented voice that said, "So sorry, madam."

Very well presented, the gentleman wore a crisp summer suit, a white shirt with an expertly tied black tie, and on his neatly styled hair (Johnny could take a lesson or two on this count), a straw hat, worn *straight*.

Samantha self-consciously patted at her hair and smoothed out her skirt. "Oh, it's quite alright." The man was handsome and charming. Why did she have to look like she was about to lose her dinner?

"So sad," he said, looking back at the scene. "I'm told she was quite talented at her job."

"You knew her?"

"Only in passing, but I really have to get back inside. Despite this tragedy, I've got work to do."

"You work at the Custom House?"

"Yes."

"What's your name?"

The man's blue eyes glinted. "I'll tell you mine, if you tell me yours."

She felt her lips tugging upward in response. "I'm Samantha Hawke, a reporter with the *Boston Daily Record*." She reached out a lacy-gloved hand and the man took it.

"Richard Wentworth. I hope we do meet again sometime, Miss Hawke."

Before Samantha could get in a professional question, Mr. Wentworth slipped away into the crowd. She closed her mouth at the stranger's obvious attempt at flirting and reprimanded herself. She was on the job! Focus!

Samantha pushed thoughts of the handsome man aside and prepared her box camera, then shot the scene until half her roll of film was used up. That done, she acquired her pencil and notepad.

"Do you know the name of the deceased?"

Samantha asked this question to no one in particular. It was rare for the police to answer when the press shouted questions, but it was something to do, and once in a while, you got lucky.

"Did she jump? Or was she pushed?"

Johnny leaped in. "C'mon, Detective Cluney, give us a crumb!"

2

Haley had seen plenty of jumping deaths before, especially during *the panic* at the end of '29, but rarely was the deceased female. The thirty-two-stories-high Custom House Tower had an observation deck on the twenty-sixth floor, but it was fenced in with wrought iron, preventing accidental or purposeful falls.

Officer Bell and a number of other police officials Haley recognized were on the scene, including Officer Jack Thompson one of the station's crime scene photographers. She and Jack had met shortly after her return to Boston in '24, she a new intern at the hospital and he a tall, ruggedly good-looking rookie beat cop. They had dated for a few months before calling it quits. They were both too dedicated to their jobs to find enough time to keep a relationship going. They'd remained friends and Haley would always be thankful for Jack's support when she'd needed it through those early days after her brother Joseph's murder and her vain effort to find his killer.

Haley was a little surprised to see Detective Emmet Cluney, the city's lead homicide detective, on the scene, though all deaths were to be considered suspicious until ruled otherwise. The beefy man was barking orders. "Officer Bell, keep those vultures behind the rope. Finch, get a blanket or something to cover the body." He paused when he saw her, and added hoarsely, "Dr. Higgins."

Haley acknowledged Detective Cluney with a nod. "Good morning, Detective. She worked here, I assume?"

"Mrs. Olivia Gray, thirty-eight, charted exported cargo. Employed at the Custom House since 1922. Her manager was so pleased with her work, that he agreed to keep her on, even though she got married during that time."

Haley lowered herself to the ground to examine the body. It wasn't a pretty sight with limbs splayed at unnatural angles, and blood pooling around the head and all visible orifices. A cursory check showed no old bruising, but there were recent markings on her hands.

Detective Cluney removed a handkerchief from his pocket, opened it to reveal a half-smoked cigar and tucked it between his lips before lighting it. After releasing a cloud of smoke, he said, "We were first alerted to a fire alarm at the building. A mass of people scurried outside and that's when the body was found."

"So, she was dispatched before the alarm was pulled?"

"Maybe she pulled it herself," Detective Cluney said, "to create a distraction? Empty her office so she'd be alone? Who knows? The fire marshal has his men running through the building now."

Haley didn't see the fire trucks, but they could have been parked on the other side of the building.

Staring skyward, she asked, "Do you know what floor she fell from?"

Most of the windows above were opened, a normal occurrence in the heat of summer.

"A Mr. Edward Tapper came forward, the first to identify the body. Said he shared an office with her on the seventh floor. He didn't see her leave when the alarm went off."

"Did he mention her state of mind?" Haley asked.

Detective Cluney shook his head. "He was pretty shook up himself. So, whatcha thinkin'? Jumper? Or murder?"

Haley rose and smoothed out her wide-legged cotton slacks. "It's hard to say. At first glance there's no evidence either way. I'll take a closer look in the lab."

Detective Cluney rocked on his heels. "My gut says jumper. More women than you'd like to think are succumbing to actual depression these days to go along with the Great Depression."

Sadly, Haley couldn't disagree.

The ambulance arrived—a boxy, whitewashed Ford van. The body was eased into a canvas bag, lifted by two strong ambulance attendants, and rolled away on the gurney. Haley frowned as flashbulbs burst from the news reporter crowd. She wasn't a fan of crime reporters, especially having been on the receiving end of their sometimes boorish behavior. They had hounded her terribly when her brother Joseph had been murdered. But that was seven years ago. Perhaps they'd become more sensitive since then.

Samantha Hawke gave her hope. Like Haley, she was a woman trying to make it in a man's world. As serendipity would have it, they'd ended up solving the last case together. Haley trusted her.

Haley watched Samantha as she wrestled with her substandard box camera. Haley had to give her new friend credit for trying. Unfortunately, Haley didn't think there was much of a story here.

"Olivia!"

A man's voice screamed above the noise of the thinning crowd. "Olivia!"

He stopped short when he reached Haley and stared at the pool of blood on the sidewalk.

He looked up with glassy eyes. "Was that... my wife?"

"Are you Mr. Gray?" Haley asked

He nodded slowly; his face pinched with dread. "I'm sorry, sir," Haley said. "She's gone."

THE BODY of Mrs. Olivia Gray lay on the cement slab under bright lights in the middle of the morgue. Haley had automatically set up for the autopsy. She was dressed in a white lab coat, had freshly washed hands, and held a sharp scalpel, preparing to make the standard Y incision.

"Hold on!" The tenor voice of an aging English man stopped her short.

Dr. Peter Guthrie, Boston's Chief Medical Examiner, held up long, gnarly fingers. "The mayor's office just rang. They wanted to remind us we're in a depression and money's tight."

Haley raised dark brows. Her boss stood in the doorway of his office, slumping slightly as men of a certain age are known to do. His white hair stood up in rebellious tufts, impervious to whatever oil products he'd bothered to use that morning. He wore a wrinkled summer suit brought from England and had finished it with a crooked bow tie. It could be obvious when interacting with widowers, just what chores and responsibilities had once landed on the wife—such as ensuring that certain grooming routines took place. Haley was tempted to pull out the tweezers and pluck the man's runaway eyebrows.

She tilted her head. "Are you saying I'm not to go ahead with this postmortem?"

"The mayor didn't say so exactly," Dr. Guthrie answered with a bony shoulder shrug, "but that was most certainly the sentiment behind his words."

"But we have to confirm the cause of death," Haley said.

"Your good detective has declared suicide."

"Yes, but we can't be sure. Besides, an autopsy could give us a clue as to why she jumped."

"I don't think the mayor really cares," Dr. Guthrie grumbled. "Whatever the reasons, knowing them won't bring her back."

Haley snorted. More often than not these days, the mayor's directives hindered her doing her job. Being professional meant being thorough and leaving questions unanswered irked her.

"I'm sorry," she murmured as she pulled the sheet over the corpse's head.

After washing up again, Haley returned to her wooden desk situated in the corner close to the door that led to the rest of the hospital. The morgue was well lit and painted white to compensate for its location in the basement. As it was part of Boston's premier hospital, it had been efficiently outfitted with the very latest forensic equipment and items needed for testing and research. At least it had been before the end of '29. Very few updates had been made since the panic set in. Haley was thankful that the decade of plenty had allowed for the acquisition of a host of modern tools, and equally thankful that Dr. Guthrie's predecessor had had the foresight to take advantage of generous budgets.

She worked on Mrs. Gray's report and put it in an envelope to be delivered to Detective Cluney. Without an autopsy, there wasn't much to write up, and the file was unusually thin. The broken bones, along with the skull impressions, were obvious, but she could only guess about the organ damage.

With that out of the way, Haley then busied herself with paperwork. She left files on her desk for her intern, Mr. Martin, to put away.

Try as she might, she couldn't get Mrs. Gray and her tragic demise out of her mind. *Why didn't the mayor want the autopsy? Was it really to save a few dollars? Or was it because the deceased was a woman?* she thought with distaste.

Was it something else?

Before she could think it through, Haley found herself at the door of Dr. Guthrie's office. A pot of tea and an empty porcelain teacup sat on his desk. His hands tented on the slight protrusion of his stomach, and his chin was bowed. He emitted a steam-engine snore in time with his rising chest.

"Dr. Guthrie?"

The man could sleep through a tornado, Haley thought. She raised her voice, "Dr. Guthrie!"

Two snorts and a loud exclamation later, Dr. Guthrie seemed to eye Haley with disdain. "Yes, what is it, Dr. Higgins?"

"I think we should do a postmortem on Mrs. Gray."

"But the mayor—"

Haley cut him off. "I know. I'll do it on my own time."

Dr. Guthrie's bushy brows formed a deep V. "It's that important to you, eh?"

"I guess it is."

"You can't file a report."

"I know."

He flapped a vein-ridden hand. "Fine, go ahead, but if the mayor finds out, it's your head."

"Thank you, Doctor."

He grunted, then said, "Before you start, get me a fresh pot of tea, will you."

Haley pivoted on her two-inch, buckled-up pumps,

and hid her scowl. Thankfully, the intern arrived at that moment. "Mr. Martin," Haley said after they'd greeted each other. "Dr. Guthrie would like a fresh pot of tea."

It was Mr. Martin's turn to scowl, but he recovered quickly and retreated to the coffee counter. Haley pitied him. "When you finish that, you can assist me with an autopsy." The skip in Mr. Martin's step returned.

Half of Mrs. Gray's face was relatively undamaged. Her bone structure indicated beauty in her youth, though time had been hard on her. The wrinkles on her face were deeper than most thirty-eight-year-old women's. Her nails were short, unpainted, but nicely manicured. Haley studied them with a magnifying glass. She saw loose skin cells on three fingers of the right hand. Hers?

Unless they belonged to an attacker?

Fresh scratches on the backs of her hands could be from hitting the edge of the window when she fell, but. . . . Haley imagined the steps necessary to jump: *edge one leg over the window sill, then the other, then with your bottom balancing on the sill and legs dangling, push off.*

Mr. Martin, scrubbed up, donned a clean lab coat, and interrupted her thoughts. "I'm ready, Dr. Higgins."

Haley smiled at his new endearment for her. "Do you want to do the honors?"

"Yes, ma'am."

"Doctor," Haley corrected.

"Sorry, Doctor. Yes, Doctor."

Haley handed him the scalpel and waited until he'd made the first incision before mentioning this post-mortem was off the clock. Haley was pleased the young man didn't mind he wouldn't be paid.

Best-case scenario, this was good practice for the young intern. Worst case, they'd find something of concern, and Haley would have to decide if a call to the mayor would be worth opening Pandora's box.

3

Samantha almost refused Johnny's offer for a ride back to the newspaper building on Water Street, but her empty change purse forced her to swallow her pride. She couldn't afford another taxi fare and walking would just make her late and damp with perspiration.

Max opened the door to the front seat of Johnny's roadster for Samantha then got into the backseat.

"Thank you, Max," Samantha said as she slid onto the leather seat. "At least there's one gentleman present."

Max blushed, and if he said something, Samantha didn't hear it.

"Oh, don't be sore, doll," Johnny said with a crooked grin that stirred Samantha's indignation. "It's not much of a story anyway. Just another jumper. Won't even make the first page."

Samantha folded her arms, jutted her chin, and stared straight ahead. That it hadn't ended up a big story wasn't the point. The issue—he had an advantage and had used it against her. If she, by some miracle, could ever afford a car one day, she certainly would not let Johnny Milwaukee step foot in it.

The breeze blew in from the opened windows. Although warm, the current of air was a welcome relief to the stifling summer heat. Not caring about the company with her, Samantha removed her hat and summer gloves.

Johnny parked in front of the three-story stone building that housed the operations of the *Boston Daily Record*. Samantha smiled sweetly and said, "Thank you for the ride, Mr. Milwaukee."

"It's my pleasure, Miss Hawke."

Inside, Samantha set her hat and gloves to the side of her desk. The room was dubbed the "pit" as it was shared between the various writers. Their desks, butting up against each other, housed Remington typewriters, black cradle telephones, dirty coffee cups, and had overused ashtrays.

They'd brought Samantha's desk in after she'd convinced her editor, Archie August, to promote her from her first position as a receptionist. Like her desk, she was an outsider in this men's club. Her phone was new, a reward from Mr. August for the part she'd played in breaking the last big story, and for her work writing it up. Samantha thought it was more of a concession to the fact that she'd nearly lost her life on the job.

Mr. August's wide girth filled the doorway of the pit. "Well? Anything?"

"Sorry, boss," Johnny answered. "Looks like it's just another jumper. A woman this time. The cops wouldn't give us any scraps. I'll keep on my contact."

Mr. August slumped thick shoulders. "Get me something for the evening papers. Anything!"

Samantha had barely unloaded her camera and messenger bag and settled herself at her desk when she sensed a presence. A sideways glance proved it to be Johnny, arrogantly leaning against her desk, his usual snide grin plastered on his face, hatless head messy, and arms crossed.

"What do you want?" She didn't even try to keep the irritation out of her voice.

"I see you like to read me?"

Samantha followed his gaze to a copy of the *Boston Daily Record* folded open to a recent story about the upcoming anniversary of a terrorist attack in Manhattan in 1916. Byline: Johnny Milwaukee.

She pushed the paper under the pile of older papers on her desk.

"I like to read the *news*. I don't care who wrote it."

Johnny smirked and picked up Samantha's favorite fountain pen.

How irresponsible to have left it on my desk. Samantha felt like ripping it from his hands.

"A Brause Iserlohn," he said with admiration. He pronounced it *icer-lawn.*

Samantha cheekily corrected him. "It's pronounced *Esser-loan.*"

"Ah, *Esserloan.* It's a beaut. Where d'you get it?"

When the paper had hired Samantha as a receptionist, her husband Seth had given his premium pen from his father to her. Seth was a louse, but he'd had his good moments. Not that it was any of Johnny's business.

"It was a gift."

"Can I borrow it?"

Samantha snatched it out of Johnny's hand. "No. It needs ink. Now, stop bothering me. Don't you have work to do?"

Johnny chuckled and strutted away. Samantha took small breaths to calm herself. She refused to let Johnny Milwaukee ruffle her feathers.

Focusing back on the Custom House death and the poor woman's demise, Samantha considered her contact at the police station, Officer Tom Bell. He'd given her the tip about the jumper, and she'd seen him at the scene. If she could get a couple of details, she could at least write up the story before Johnny. Better than nothing.

She picked up her heavy receiver, dialed, then turned her back on the others. Freddy Hall, a brooding, middle-aged sports reporter, was easily annoyed because of her gender, and she didn't want him or the guys to overhear.

When the operator answered, she asked to be connected.

"Officer Tom Bell."

"Hello, Officer Bell," Samantha said. She imagined the officer using the station telephone. He was slim, average height, and wore his blue police uniform with a police hat resting firmly on his blond head. "It's Miss Hawke, from the *Boston Daily Record*."

She heard a soft sigh from the other end.

"What can I do for you, *Miss Hawke?*"

Samantha and Tom Bell had a sort of camaraderie. She'd saved his life, which put them on a first-name basis. Tom had made it clear he was interested in more than simple friendship, but Samantha couldn't and wouldn't go beyond that, not while she was still officially married to Seth. And when at work she preferred to keep things professional.

"I want to thank you again for the tip about the jumper. Do you have any more information?"

"I've gotta name."

A thrill rushed through her. "You do? What is it?"

"Mrs. Olivia Gray. An employee of the Custom House."

"Married employee?"

"Apparently. Not sure if her boss knew. He's coming in soon to make a statement."

What I'd give to be a fly on the wall for that, Samantha thought.

"What about her husband? Is he still alive?" It would explain how a married woman could be employed there. There wasn't a law against hiring married women—yet companies seriously frowned upon it.

"Yup, but appears to be of a weak constitution."

"What do you mean?"

"He fainted when he heard the news, and now he's catatonic."

"Poor man."

"Yeah. He's here. The boss won't let him walk 'til he talks, so I hope he loosens his yapper soon," Tom said.

"Anything else? Anyone know why she did it?"

"We're only guessing at the moment. She's got a kid. Her coworker, a Mr. Philip Snow, is in shock. He can't believe she'd leave her son, but we've seen many ladies leave kids behind. Think they're doing 'em a favor."

"Was anyone left in the building when Mrs. Gray jumped?" Samantha asked. "Any witnesses?"

"Each floor is assigned a janitor, but they, like pretty much everyone else, clogged the stairwell in their effort to get out. No one much liked the idea of getting caught in a fire in such a tall building."

Samantha made a small sound of agreement. *Imagine getting stuck on one of the higher floors with a raging fire blocking the way out.*

Is that what Mrs. Gray had thought? That fire blocked her from her exit and she had no choice?

No, that would've been too extreme. There wasn't even any smoke, much less imminent fire danger.

"Thanks, Tom, uh, Officer Bell. I appreciate it."

Samantha hung up and started typing. It wasn't much, but it was more than Johnny had. He'd been too busy smoking cigarettes and talking with Freddy Hall about the unassisted double play by Pittsburgh Pirates' outfielder Adam Comorosky in a recent ballgame against the New York Giants to bother picking up his telephone. Samantha couldn't stop a soft grin from tickling her red lips. If she were extra lucky, she might have a decent shot with her box camera to go with the story.

. . .

It wasn't uncommon for Haley to put in long days. Her field of choice fascinated her. Whether reading textbooks and the latest forensic science magazines or getting her hands dirty on the operating table, she'd get lost in her work, and time seemed to liquefy.

From the corner of her eye, she noticed that the intern had turned a concerning shade of green. She set her full gaze on him.

"Are you all right, Mr. Martin?"

He cleared his voice. "I'm fine. But, uh, would you mind if I got a drink of water?"

Haley nodded, giving the young man leave, and she returned to the task at hand. The chest cavity of Mrs. Gray was open and the organs exposed. The damage from a fall of that height was extreme, and it wasn't possible to do the usual weighing and measuring. There were no visible signs of any pre-existing diseases, however, there was old bruising on both wrists and arms. Haley had seen bruising like this before. Someone in the last week or so had grabbed and handled the victim roughly.

Haley found the brain tissue compromised, which made it difficult to tell if the visible blood clots had been there before the fall. A brain ailment could point to a probable accidental fall. *Windows were normally opened. The summer months had been muggy and hot.*

If Mrs. Gray had grown woozy, she might've leaned too far over the edge.

When Haley tried to imagine that scenario, the physics didn't work. *Unless the lower pane were below Mrs. Gray's center of gravity, she wouldn't have tumbled out. She would've collapsed to the floor.*

Mr. Martin walked back to the table, his color having returned to his cheeks.

"Please sew her up," Haley instructed, "and take blood samples to the lab."

"Yes, Dr. Higgins."

Haley washed her hands and returned to her desk to write up her report. Perhaps Dr. Guthrie and the mayor had been right, and she'd just completed a fool's errand.

Yet something bothered her.

She picked up the telephone receiver and called the police station.

"Connect me to Detective Cluney, please."

As Haley waited, she mulled over the case. *Fall from seven floors—severe head trauma. Broken neck, two broken clavicles, shattered humerus and radius on each arm, and every rib cracked.*

"Cluney here!"

"Detective Cluney, it's Dr. Higgins."

"What are you still doing at work?"

"What are *you* still doing at work?" Haley

returned. The detective had a family waiting. If anyone should've called it a day, it was him.

"Working," Detective Cluney answered. "What can I do for you?"

"I'm calling about the Olivia Gray case."

"The jumper? What about it?"

"I don't think she jumped."

Haley could hear the detective puff on his cigar and let out a long breath. He finally responded, "Why's that?"

"All the major damage is above the waist. Severe damage to the skull, neck broken, both collar bones snapped, major breaks in both arms, every single rib cracked. It was like she was hung upside down and dropped."

"She fell from the seventh floor and probably did a somersault midair."

Haley couldn't picture it, but there was only one way to find out.

"Is there an officer on site?"

"Nope. No reason. There's night security on duty."

"Could you get someone to call to give me access to the scene?"

Haley could sense the detective tense. "What for?"

"I'd like to perform an experiment."

Detective Cluney honored Haley's request and arranged for an officer to speak to the security guard on her behalf. She found the middle-aged guard waiting as she and Mr. Martin pulled up to the Custom House in her 1929 DeSoto in the early evening hours.

Haley wouldn't call Emmet Cluney a friend, but they shared a mutual respect for one another, even with Detective Cluney's rough-around-the-edges demeanor. They'd first worked together when Haley had returned from London seven years ago, after her brother's brutal murder.

Unfortunately, the Joseph Higgins case had grown cold, but she and Detective Cluney had cooperated on many other cases over the years, some of which had ended with a conviction.

"Dr. Higgins," the dark-suited security guard said. "I can take you upstairs."

"We have an object to bring with us. It's rather heavy."

"Do you require a trolley, Doctor?"

"That would be perfect."

Haley opened the trunk of her car, and when the guard arrived with the trolley, she grinned at his bemused expression.

"A body, Dr. Higgins? I had expected boxes."

4

"It's a dummy, Mr. Patterson." Haley shared a look with her intern who appeared to hold in a grin.

Mr. Patterson hemmed and hawed. "I see." Then as if dummies were delivered to the Custom House every day he asked, "Is it fragile?"

Using the morgue's teaching skeleton and several bags of sand Mr. Martin had collected from the docks, they'd stitched the gunny sacks together as a type of skin for the skeleton. They'd filled the sacks with sand, evenly distributed, until it weighed the same as Mrs. Gray, roughly 130 pounds.

The sandbags wouldn't be strong enough to protect the skeleton, which was why Haley had brought Mr. Martin even though she would have preferred to do the experiment herself. As long as it provided an educational experience for her intern, it justified the skeleton being damaged.

Haley answered the guard. "The stitching might give if we're not careful."

Mr. Martin assisted Haley as they moved the dummy onto the trolley while Mr. Patterson strapped it on. The guard pushed it toward the elevator, and Haley and Mr. Martin followed.

Mr. Patterson pushed the 7 button. Without speaking, they stood facing the door, listening to the gears groan and clang until they reached their floor. Mr. Patterson opened the metal gate then led the way while Mr. Martin pushed the dummy to Olivia Gray's office. Mr. Patterson retrieved a key from his pocket and opened the door.

"Is there anything else, you'll be needing, Dr. Higgins? he asked.

"No. Mr. Martin and I can manage now."

"Very well. I'll let you out of the building when you're ready."

"Thank you, Mr. Patterson."

"Uh, one more thing, if you don't mind," he said as he looked over his shoulder. "Are you going to throw the dummy out of the window?"

Haley nodded. "We are."

"Then I'll arrange for a clean up."

Haley flicked the light switch. The office contained three desks, all turned toward each other. It was apparent which one belonged to Mrs. Gray because a woman's sweater hung on the back of the chair. Detective Cluney had mentioned the other two occupants were Mr. Snow and Mr. Tapper. Unlike the other desks, Mrs. Gray's was cleared off and tidy. A fine layer of dust had settled on the surface, a common occurrence for most dwellings in the summer. The dust of the dry roads got kicked up by a growing number of automobiles.

There was no evidence of the black dust used for identifying fingerprints, though the drawers were cracked open, and her filing cabinet papers askew—evidence the police had done a cursory search. Detective Cluney hadn't mentioned finding anything of note.

The police photographer had taken plenty of pictures of the scene, but Haley didn't know if they'd bothered to snap any from the office. She'd brought her camera and forensic kit. Handing the camera to Mr. Martin, she instructed, "Take as many pictures as you can."

"Of what?"

"Mrs. Gray's desk, the window, the window sill, and the street view." Haley hoped the long summer day still cast enough light for the exposure to be successful. "Pay special attention to the area where the body landed."

Mr. Martin adjusted the camera and snapped. The smoke from the flash pans made Haley cough, and she opened the window wide.

Haley always kept a fingerprint kit in her forensic bag. After dusting Mrs. Gray's desk for prints, she didn't know what she hoped to find since many people had been through this office and touched Mrs. Gray's desk. Better to have the prints and not need them than to want them and not have them.

"You don't think she jumped, do you, Dr. Higgins?" Mr. Martin said as he moved about the room.

"I'm not sure. That's why we're here. To see if we *can* be sure."

"Have you always wanted to be a pathologist, Dr. Higgins?"

Haley stilled for a moment before dusting the back of Mrs. Gray's chair.

"I've always wanted to be a doctor. Having grown up on a farm, I first thought I'd be a veterinarian, but then the Great War started, and I served as a nurse. For a while, though I was always intrigued with forensic science, I thought I'd be a doctor in the traditional sense, but then—"

"Then what?"

Joe died. As if looking to escape, Haley glanced at the door. "Then I decided I like to work with people who don't ask questions," Haley said with a smile.

Mr. Martin took the hint.

Once Mr. Martin had completed the photographs and the desk had been brushed for fingerprints, Haley asked her intern if he was ready.

"Yes, I am."

"Great." Haley pushed the trolley to the opened window. "I need you to help me lift it."

"We're just going to toss it out?"

"No. We're going to throw it out as if the dummy were making a jump."

"Why?"

"Do you remember the autopsy, Mr. Martin?"

"Massive damage to the torso and head." The light of understanding flashed behind his eyes. "Very little damage to the legs and feet. If she'd jumped, it would be the other way around, wouldn't it?"

"That's the theory we're here to test." Haley wished she had two dummies, one to push and one to drop on its head, but this would have to do. They propped the dummy up against the wall, then Haley retrieved two chairs. "You stand on one, and I'll stand on one. Together we can lift it and, to the best of our ability, make it 'jump.'"

As Haley instructed, they propped up the dummy and lifted one leg over the windowsill. Haley pushed the other leg over, and they let it fall.

5

Samantha's tired legs felt as if they weighed a ton as she lugged herself up the grimy steps of her tenement building and down the dimly lit hallway to her second-floor apartment she shared with her six-year-old daughter, Talia, and her mother-in-law, Bina. The mingled smells of greasy meals and cheap cigarettes made her feel vaguely nauseous.

What Samantha hated most about the tenements —besides the stench, the leaky pipes, and the cramped living space—was the lack of privacy. Everyone knew everybody's business. The Langs' infant son was crying again, probably another earache and no medicine to relieve the pain; hard-of-hearing old Mrs. MacDonald's radio show bled through the thin walls; another argument had erupted between Seamus and Sylvia O'Connor, Seamus's voice bellowing, "If you don't do as I say, woman, I'll beat you again!"

Samantha grimaced. What fresh bruising would she see on Mrs. O'Connor's face the next time they passed each other in the hall? What new excuse would she give? She hardly had enough doors to walk into, and no one could be as clumsy as Sylvia O'Connor claimed to be.

Fishing her key out of her messenger bag, Samantha let herself into her apartment and announced, "I'm home!" With a tired sigh, she shrugged off the well-used messenger bag and box camera from her shoulder. She'd barely gotten her hat and gloves off and put away on the rack behind the door when Talia came barreling toward her.

"Mommy!"

Samantha scooped her daughter into her arms. "Hi, honey. I missed you!"

"I missed you too," Talia's round blue eyes blinked up at her. "Mommy, why can't you stay home like the other mommies?"

Samantha's heart lurched. How she wished she could! Even though she liked her job, the hours were long, and it was not like she had a choice anyway. Lousy Seth Rosenbaum had stolen that when he'd ditched his responsibilities as a husband and father and taken off. Samantha didn't hope the man was dead in a pit on the side of the road—she wasn't that spiteful—but that didn't mean she had to wish him well either.

She forced a smile and kissed Talia's honey-blond head. "I'm here now, and I'm all yours."

She carried her lightweight daughter into the living room and settled onto a threadbare divan. Across from them were two mismatched armchairs and a scratched coffee table. Cream and green floral-print wallpaper rebelled by pulling away at the corners.

Bina wouldn't stand for a speck of dirt and kept the small apartment immaculate. Samantha suspected the rigorous cleaning schedule the older woman put herself through was a way to keep her mind from focusing on her losses—first a husband, then a son. There had been other children, but they'd died in infancy or at birth. Bina refused to talk about them. Samantha couldn't blame her for holding on to the bitterness, though it hadn't made the woman any happier.

The kitchen opened into the living area and Bina, standing with her bony hands on narrow hips, said, "Finally." The wooden table was set, a chore Samantha usually did with Talia, and a pot of something sat in the middle. "The stew is getting cold. We can't exactly afford to have the stove going all night to keep supper warm."

Bina Rosenbaum wore her white hair pulled into a

severe bun and carried herself with a slight hump in her shoulders. Her frail look deceived those who didn't know her. What she lacked in physical strength, she made up for with a sharp tongue. "I don't understand why you're getting home later all the time. What will the neighbors think?"

Samantha didn't give one red cent what the neighbors thought. She answered tersely, "I can't help my hours." They had this argument often. "It's the nature of the job." She took Talia's hand and led her to the kitchen.

Not easily mollified, Bina said, "What? Sitting around all day playing with a typewriter?"

Samantha huffed. "I don't sit around all day *playing* with a typewriter. I *work* with a typewriter. And I don't sit around all day either."

She was tempted to shock Bina with tales of the horrific death she'd witnessed that morning. She hadn't spent the afternoon testing perfumes at Sears as she did for the ladies' pages she wrote, but she held her tongue. Talia was present, and besides, Samantha was just too tired to get into another verbal sparring session.

Instead, she and Talia washed their hands in the kitchen sink and then took their places at the table. Bina started the *brachah rishonah,* and Samantha inhaled deeply. She found the prayer to be calming, which was what she needed right now.

With closed eyes and folded hands, Bina recited, "*Barukh ata Adonai Eloheinu, Melekh ha'olam, shehakol nih'ye bidvaro.* Blessed are You, Lord our God, King of the Universe, through whose word everything comes into being."

The results of Haley's experiment looped in her mind, so she didn't notice that when she entered her fourth-story, top-floor apartment on Grove Street she had company. She deposited her purse and hat on the sideboard before crossing through the opened French doors into the living room. Her jaw dropped for a split second before she composed herself.

It was after dusk, so the lamps cast a warm glow over the room. The high-ceiling walls were papered and trimmed with decorative molding. Along with a four-foot-tall Areca palm, stood a handsome, polished floor radio. Mr. Midnight was curled up on one of the plush maroon armchairs. When he saw Haley, he stood on his three legs—he had come to them via the fire escape, wet and scrawny in the middle of the night, his missing leg a mystery—and stretched out his back in a deep arch. He greeted Haley by rubbing his black fur against her cream-colored slacks, before hiking to the kitchen in his classic three-legged, rabbit-like step-hop, where his food bowl sat.

Haley's kind-hearted housekeeper and companion, Molly McPhail, sat on one end of the couch. She balanced a teacup and saucer on her soft lap, her round cheeks rosy and her eyebrow raised in question. Across from her sat the object of Haley's shock and growing mortification.

"Dr. Guthrie?"

"Nice of you to join us, Dr. Higgins."

"I'm so sorry." She glanced appealingly at Molly. "Was that tonight?"

"Yes, Dr. Higgins."

"Oh dear." Haley lowered herself into a vacant armchair—one not covered in black cat fur. Molly had reminded her that morning that Dr. Guthrie would be joining them for supper. She'd created an undeniably awkward situation for Molly and her new boss. "I can't believe I forgot. I'm so very sorry. Have you eaten already?"

"Of course not," Molly said with a note of reproach in her voice. Haley understood. It would be highly inappropriate for the housekeeper to dine alone with a guest as distinguished as the Chief Medical Examiner.

"I'm happy you've had a chance to meet," Haley continued lightly and began official, if belated, introductions. "Dr. Guthrie, Miss McPhail came to me as a housekeeper when I returned to Boston in twenty-four but has become a close friend since. I consider her a companion now. Molly, Dr. Guthrie and I met several years ago back in England while working on a case together."

This part Molly knew since Haley had gone into great detail about the many idiosyncrasies the new chief possessed.

"Miss McPhail has done a splendid job of keeping me occupied in your absence," Dr. Guthrie said. His voice retained its baritone gruffness, but his eyes were soft as his gaze returned to Molly.

Dr. Guthrie's actions surprised Haley. She hadn't seen an iota of gentleness, or interest in anything other than taking tea and working on crossword puzzles, since the Englishman had arrived at the morgue. Then again, Molly had a way of making people at ease.

"Shall we eat?" Molly asked. "The roast is in the oven. I've basted it a couple of times, so it should still be moist."

"Yes, yes," Haley said quickly. They often ate late in the evening, but she sincerely hoped her tardiness and absentmindedness hadn't ruined Molly's efforts to impress their guest.

Haley offered Dr. Guthrie the head of the sturdy wooden table already set and then helped Molly carry the roast and braised vegetables to the table. Wishing she could have a glass of wine as she would've done in

England, Haley knew that in New England they would have to settle for grape juice.

Haley sat beside their guest and across from Molly. She was about to lift her glass and announce, "Bon Appetit" when Molly spoke.

"Would you like to say grace, Dr. Guthrie?"

"Molly—" Haley started. She didn't know if Dr. Guthrie was religious and if he were, she assumed he'd be protestant. Molly was firmly Catholic.

Dr. Guthrie surprised Haley again. "I'd be happy to, Miss McPhail." He further shocked Haley by reciting the Catholic prayer. She listened with head bowed as Molly and Dr. Guthrie prayed together, "Bless us, oh Lord for these thy gifts that we have received from thy bounty, through Christ our Lord, Amen."

This was followed by a synchronized signing of the cross. Haley bit her lip when a very odd and entirely inappropriate thought crossed her mind. *These two would make a cute couple!*

Once they'd passed the dishes around and filled their plates, and both she and Dr. Guthrie had praised the meal and thanked the cook, Haley repeated her apologies.

"I want to explain why I was late tonight," she said. "You'll find this of particular interest, Dr. Guthrie."

"Proceed," he said.

"As you know, I did an unauthorized autopsy on Mrs. Gray."

"That's the Custom House jumper?" Molly asked.

"Yes," Haley answered. "Except, I don't think she jumped."

Both Molly and Dr. Guthrie stilled, forks stabbed with roast beef hovering in the air. Haley filled them both in on her findings.

"Mr. Martin and I made a dummy, took it to Mrs. Gray's office, and recreated the jump."

"And . . ." Dr. Guthrie said.

"The legs of the skeleton shattered with some fracturing of the torso. The skull sustained some damage but not nearly what our victim suffered. Mrs. Gray's injuries support a head-first fall. Not only that, I found skin under the victim's fingernails and fresh scratches on the back of her hands that could indicate a struggle."

"Have you let Detective Cluney know?" Molly asked.

"Yes. I called him from the morgue." Haley looked apologetically at Dr. Guthrie. "I returned the skeletal remains. I'm afraid there's quite a lot of damage, but Mr. Martin has promised to glue it together tomorrow."

Dr. Guthrie snorted. "So long as the fellow learned something from the exercise."

Haley smiled in relief. "I believe he did."

After they had finished supper and Dr. Guthrie had left, Haley helped Molly clean up the kitchen then took a cup of tea to her office.

The room held an elegant wooden desk, a plush velvet desk chair, a set of floor-to-ceiling shelves filled with books, and on the wooden floor, a length of green carpet, which angled upward slightly to a cup in the middle of one end. Propped up in one corner, her golf bag sported an array of clubs. Haley retrieved a putting iron and a ball. She found the exercise relaxing. The need to focus her body and mind's attention on one small task overwhelmed her. Focusing on putting the ball into the cup relaxed her.

Once she felt her stress levels taper off, she took a seat at her desk. A tap at the door, and Molly poked her head into the office.

"I made a pot of tea and thought you'd like a cup."

"Thank you, Molly."

Haley blew on the delicious English tea while opening the file that had become a permanent fixture on her desk: Joe's case.

She picked up the photographs, one by one.

Joe is on the ground in a bad part of town. He lies on the stained sidewalk. Litter is stuffed in crannies up to the foundation of the nearest brick building. There is blood on his neck, though the stab wound is hard to see.

The bruising under his eyes looks like shadows. His fists are hidden under his body.

Haley had seen his corpse and knew his fists had been bruised as well, but they weren't recent bruises—not from the struggle that had occurred at his death.

Haley placed the pictures back into the file and removed a newspaper article about backroom gambling and bare-fist fighting—both illegal activities, then and now.

Sighing, Haley returned the clipping. She hated to think that her brother had been involved in such illicit and dangerous affairs, but she couldn't rule it out. And no one she'd asked had been willing to talk. No one seemed to know anything about her brother. The room he'd rented had been bare—only dirty clothing and sheets on the cot that could've belonged to anyone.

It was as if he were a ghost and had never existed. As though someone had wanted to make sure he was erased.

6

"Who is this?"

Samantha stared at the receiver in her hand as it emitted a loud dial tone. She pondered the message. The female tipster sounded young, or perhaps she was an older person altering her voice. Whoever it was must've been referring to the Custom House jumper. Had the caller seen something? Was there a witness to a crime? A murder?

Her gaze moved upward. Johnny was staring at her. *Drat, that man! He was like a cobra ready to pounce.* Samantha shrugged as if the telephone call had been nothing and mouthed, "*wrong number.*"

Butterflies fluttered in her chest. There *was* a story here. If only she could identify the caller, but unless the gal called again, Samantha would never know who she was.

She wouldn't find anything out by just sitting here. She cleared off her desk and locked the page of her unfinished story in her desk.

"That was, uh, I have to go," she said to no one, but sharp-eared Johnny heard.

"I thought you said it was a wrong number."

"You misheard me. I said a friend. Not that it's any of your beeswax."

Grabbing her bag and camera, Samantha raced out of the building down the sidewalk and around the corner. She caught her breath as she braced herself against the wall, then risked a peek. Sure enough, Johnny stood on the front steps, looking for her. She ducked out of sight and bit her lip to keep from grinning too smugly. No way was she going to let him profit from her lead and take all the glory.

Now free from Johnny's prying eyes, Samantha was at a loss about what to do next. She snorted. *He would know what to do.*

No, she could do this. She was a bona fide investigative reporter with the *Boston Daily Record.* She could figure this out on her own.

Maybe it would help to go back to the scene. If the caller had seen something, she'd be from around the area—maybe she had been walking home from the store.

Samantha walked quickly down Milk Street toward McKinley Square, only stopping when she reached the place where Mrs. Gray's body had been found.

The police rope was gone and cleaners had mopped the stains on the sidewalk. India Street was empty compared to the previous day. The magnificence of the building rose before her. Large Grecian pillars surrounded the exterior of the old Custom House, and the new tower, like a grand Egyptian obelisk, poked the sky at a dizzying height.

Life went on. It was almost as if Mrs. Gray's last day had never happened.

Samantha's shoulders slumped. What had she hoped to find, anyway? If the witness had been so careful as to disguise her voice and hang up before Samantha could question her further, she wasn't exactly about to run over and reveal herself now.

Which begged the question: why had she called Samantha? There were plenty more seasoned reporters, men mostly. Was that why? Had her mystery caller purposely sought her out because she wanted to tell a woman?

Deep in thought, Samantha didn't see the pedestrian in front of her before she bumped into him.

"Oh, it's you," she said.

The dapper gentleman who'd bumped into her the day before turned. Samantha smiled, gaining control of herself and the situation. "We have to stop meeting like this, Mr. Wentworth."

The mischievous glint in his gaze returned. "I don't know about that, Miss Hawke."

Mr. Wentworth *was* flirting with her! Samantha felt herself blush. Denying the man's charm was hard.

"What's it like to work at the Custom House, Mr. Wentworth?"

He shrugged one shoulder and lifted his gaze. "It's a pleasant place to spend one's day. I have to say, it's quite a grand specimen of American architecture."

"I was here when they built it in 1913," Samantha said. "Just a child when it was finished in fifteen, but I remember being in absolute awe. It was unbelievably tall, like something out of a fairy tale."

Mr. Wentworth chuckled. "I would've liked to have seen it go up."

"I'm guessing you grew up in England?"

"London, as a matter of fact."

"Do you miss it?"

"Boston is very much like home, but with the bonus of being in America, the land of opportunity. Now your turn, what's it like to be a reporter?"

He quickly raised a palm, stopping Samantha

before she could speak. "Before you answer, I will admit I have never met a female investigative reporter before. I'm quite intrigued. Miss Hawke, I know we've just met, but would you consider having dinner with me tonight?"

7

Slow days at the paper, which sadly happened often, afforded Samantha time to work on the ladies' pieces she had promised to submit to Mr. August each week. She liked to divide her columns up between Fashion Tips When Pinching Pennies, Delicious Meals on a Dime, Housekeeping in a Hurry, and Social Events.

Samantha was working on the latest make-up product from Maybelline—*Try Maybelline eye shadow and eyebrow pencil to make your eyes look larger and more interesting!* She couldn't help but take a moment to sneak a peek into her compact mirror. Thin-line eyebrows were murder to keep in check. And darn painful at that! She didn't blame women for simply shaving them off and drawing them on instead.

Savage—a new kind of dry rouge. Actually stays on all day . . . or all night.

Even though her fingers zipped at sixty words a minute, her thoughts moved from make-up tricks to her unhappy neighbors. She'd bumped into Sylvia O'Connor in the hallway that morning as the poor woman shuffled four of her six kids out the door for school. Soon summer break would start, and kids would be wreaking havoc in the building. Samantha didn't know how Mrs. O'Connor did it. Especially with a violent husband.

There was a new bruise on the woman's face. Samantha pretended not to notice since mentioning it would only embarrass her beleaguered neighbor, and nothing Samantha could do or say would help her. Mrs. O'Connor was a slave to her circumstances. She loved her children and would die before leaving them. Samantha just hoped Seamus O'Connor wouldn't kill her first.

Samantha's fingers paused over her typewriter keys. Maybe there was something she could do for Mrs. O'Connor. Maybe not directly, but indirectly, and other women like her. Samantha had the power of the pen, or in this case, the typewriter.

She could write about the plight of the abused woman. Bring domestic violence to public awareness. Maybe be a catalyst for change. The rush of a story bubbled inside, and she bounded out of her seat, crossed the floor of the pit, passed the framed picture of a distinguished-looking Abraham Lincoln, and went right into Mr. August's office.

"Absolutely not!"

Samantha was stunned. "Why not?"

"It's too controversial for the ladies' pages." The editor made a show of clipping his cigar and lighting it. He spoke as he let out a stream of blue smoke from the corner of his chapped lips. "Besides, I'd have a riot on my hands. Husbands would be knocking down my door for a lynching."

"Are you kidding me? Wife battery is against the law."

"Yeah, so is imbibing alcohol. Neither is enforced all that well."

Mr. August's head bobbed up at her apparent audacity.

She quietly added, "Sir."

"Look here, Miss Hawke. I know you've had a taste of notoriety—"

"It's not that. The battering of women is a real social problem." When disinterest flashed behind the heavy-set man's eyes, Samantha tried a different approach. "You always say controversy sells papers. Let me write it as an open letter to the editor. I'll use a pseudonym, so no one will know it's internal. Imagine all the letters that will come in. You know how people like to buy papers if they think their name will be printed."

Mr. August sat back in his chair—halfway in thought—his eyes shuttering closed.

Samantha had seen this look before, and she held her breath.

"Okay," Mr. August finally said as he opened his eyes. "But if it backfires, I'll have your head."

Samantha hoped he meant that figuratively. "Thank you, Mr. August." She left before the big man had a chance to change his mind.

Back in the pit, Samantha failed to remove her look of victory from her face before Johnny noticed. He sauntered over with a suave expression, chin ducked, and fists in the pockets of his trousers. Samantha squared her shoulders.

"You're like the snake who got the mouse," he said. "C'mon, spill the beans."

"No beans here," Samantha said smugly. It felt good to be the one with a work secret for a change.

He leaned over her shoulder. "Pretty please with honey on top."

No matter how much charm her coworker piled on, she would never give up her bounty. She pushed him away. "Step back!"

"Fine." Johnny held his hands in the air in feigned surrender. "It can't be worth much, anyway."

"What makes you say that?"

"You're still here, aren't ya? If you had a big lead, you'd be flying out the door with your bag and cute little Kodak."

Samantha scowled at his slight on her box camera.

"Don't you have anything better to do, Johnny? Go back to your desk. Some of us have to work."

Samantha rolled a fresh piece of crisp white paper into her typewriter. She pulled the handle, which pushed the carriage to the left, and set her fingers on home row. She waited for inspiration to strike.

Wife battering is a social blight on our soc—

No. She pulled the carriage return lever twice to a new line.

Women are the silent victims in many homes. Where they should be loved and protected, they are scared and abused.

Samantha sighed. That felt wrong too. Maybe her approach was wrong. She was supposed to be an anonymous contributor, right? The letter should sound like it was from a battered woman. Samantha tried to put herself in Sylvia O'Connor's shoes.

I'm covered in bruises, and this at the hand of my husband, the man who vowed to honor and protect me. Don't tell me I should go to the police, because, you know what will happen? He'll get a slap on the wrist for "wife battery," and then he'll kick me to the curb. Literally. He'll get the kids, the furniture, everything, and what will happen to me? I'll be living a new kind of hell, selling my body at the docks. So, don't stare at me with your pity. Don't stare at me at all.

Samantha's throat clogged with emotion as she typed these words. She finally understood Mrs. O'Connor's blank stares and her willingness to do nothing.

Samantha hadn't felt so helpless in a coon's age. She hoped this letter got people talking!

She signed it with a flourish, *Mrs. Black and Blue.*

The ringing of her telephone startled her, and she stared at it as though she didn't know what the instrument was for. It continued to ring, and she answered it.

"Please hold for an incoming call."

Samantha waited until the line was connected. "Sam Hawke here."

"I saw what happened," a small voice said. "She didn't jump."

WHEN A KNOCK SOUNDED from the door of the morgue, Haley nodded toward Mr. Martin. "Can you get that?"

Thomas Martin put the bottle of glue and a fragmented section of the teaching skeleton aside and let Miss Hawke in.

"Hello, Samantha," Haley said. She wasn't surprised her reporter friend had stopped by, only that it had taken her this long to do so.

Samantha stepped inside. "Am I interrupting?"

"Not at all. I imagine you want to discuss the death of Mrs. Gray?"

"I do if you don't mind."

"Come on in."

Haley plugged in the electric kettle for coffee and prepared a French press with a mound of dry grounds.

"Coffee, Mr. Martin?" she called out. She didn't bother asking Dr. Guthrie—a dedicated tea man—and "resting" at his office desk.

"No, thanks, Dr. Higgins," Mr. Martin said. His attention was focused on repairing the skeleton that was in a couple of small piles on one of the morgue tables.

"What happened to it?" Samantha asked.

"We dropped it off the seventh floor of the tower."

"You don't say. What on earth for?"

"I'm not convinced Mrs. Gray's death was suicide."

"Me neither."

Haley handed Samantha a steaming mug and returned to her desk. "And why is that?"

"I got an anonymous tip. A girl or a lady

pretending to be a girl called me at the paper. All she said was 'I saw what happened. She didn't jump.' Then she hung up."

"Interesting."

"Officer Bell told me everyone left via the stairwell after someone pulled the fire alarm. Yet my tipster said she saw Mrs. Gray, and whatever happened to her. Someone must have lagged behind."

Haley mulled this piece of news over. "Have you told the police?"

"Huh?"

"About your tipster."

Samantha stilled, her mug of coffee holding steady in midair. "You know, I didn't even think about that. I probably should've, eh? But I work in a pit, and the surrounding hounds would be all over this if I made a call from there. It's dog eat dog, ya know. And we women usually end up at the bottom of the pile."

Before Haley could press the issue, Samantha changed the subject.

"Tell me about your skeleton." When Haley hesitated, she added, "Hey, I told you my lead."

Haley considered her new friend. She and Miss Hawke had been through an ordeal together, and it was normal for relationships that formed in a crisis to seem closer than perhaps they really were. But she liked

Samantha Hawke, and if she could help her out, she would.

"I became suspicious when I performed the autopsy on Mrs. Gray. Her injuries pointed to a fall occurring head and shoulders first, with a probable initial struggle. Mr. Martin and I built a dummy to test out my theory."

"And . . ."

"The injuries our skeleton obtained, having been dropped feet first, weren't consistent with Mrs. Gray's."

Samantha whistled. "Wow. That's brilliant."

Haley thought it was only reasonable science, but she accepted the praise graciously.

"What should we do now?" Samantha asked.

Haley raised a brow. "About?"

"About solving this case?"

"First thing we do is call Detective Cluney. I've yet to report my findings as well."

Haley had been hesitant to do so as her experiment wasn't foolproof, but now, with a possible witness, her hypothesis would be taken more seriously.

"Do you think you could do it?" Samantha said. "The press isn't exactly welcome at the station . . ."

Haley eyed her friend. "And you don't want to run into Officer Bell."

"No, it's not . . . well, it is a bit awkward between

us. I do like him, but it's not, you know, the right time for it. Besides, I have to keep some things close to my chest. Otherwise, the dogs at the office will gobble it up, and me with it. There's a reason they call where I work the 'pit.'"

"I understand the pressure of competition. Yours, in particular, I imagine, can be grueling."

Samantha let out a noticeable sigh of relief. "Thank you for understanding." She then grew quiet and introspective and attempted to sip from an empty cup.

"Would you like more?" Haley asked.

"No, I'm fine. It's just. . ."

"Just what?

"A man I barely know asked me out to dinner."

Haley's dark brow arched dramatically. "Really?"

Samantha's eyes hinted at embarrassment. "I ran into him twice in two days, both times while I was in front of the Custom House. He works there." She looked Haley in the eyes. "You know, it feels like serendipity."

"What about the fact that you're married?" Haley asked. It wasn't a judgment. Samantha had confided in her she didn't feel it was right to see other men, even though she pretended for her job's sake to be single.

"How long am I expected to wait for Seth? Talia hasn't even met her father, for Pete's sake. For all I know, he's dead. I'll turn into an old maid if I keep at it."

Haley chuckled, and Samantha blushed with mortification. "Oh, Haley, I'm so sorry. I didn't mean—"

"It's fine. I know my age and my social status, and I'm fine with it. Have you thought about petitioning for a death ruling? Do you have any proof he's come to an unfortunate end?"

Samantha shook her head. "Nothing concrete."

"Well, it's been seven years, hasn't it?" Haley said, remembering their earlier conversations. "You don't have to prove your husband is dead if no one's had contact with him. He will be presumed dead."

Samantha blinked. "Just like that?"

"Just like that."

"It's a lot to process. I feel like I should do something to make it official."

Samantha shifted her weight and crossed her legs. "Anyway, I said no to Mr. Wentworth for dinner, but he persisted, and now we're meeting for lunch tomorrow. I'll use the time to ask questions about the Custom House and who might've lagged after the alarm. A wayward janitor, or something. Somebody there knows something."

Haley had an idea. "Where are you meeting? I

could take a table next to you and listen in. Would you mind?"

Samantha laughed. "A real reconnaissance mission, huh? Sure. But if there's a second date, I'm doing that alone."

8

The Gray family lived in a second-floor apartment facing the Charles River. Balancing a box of doughnuts in one hand, Haley knocked on the door. She wouldn't have been surprised if there had been no answer—the man might've left Boston, or gotten a bit of work as some men found distraction a better way to deal with grief, but just when she was about to give up, the door cracked open.

"Mr. Gray?" Haley asked. The man's hair was dry and uncombed, his face unshaven and shadowed with bristles. His nose and cheeks were a blotchy red.

He spoke in a clipped voice tinged with an Eastern European accent. "I'm done talking to the press."

"I'm not with the papers, Mr. Gray. I'm Dr. Higgins, the assistant chief medical examiner. I did the autopsy on your wife. I came to offer my condolences."

She held out the box of doughnuts.

Mr. Gray eyed the offering with suspicion and frowned. "I didn't ask for no autopsy. Don't you dare send me no bill!"

"The cost of the autopsy has been covered," Haley said, keeping her voice even. "I would like to discuss my findings with you if you'd be willing to invite me inside?"

The door widened as Mr. Gray shuffled backward, his face twisting as though he were in pain.

"Are you all right, Mr. Gray?"

"Yes. Damn war injury is all. Shrapnel still in my leg."

"Forgive my intrusion," Haley continued. "I won't be long."

"I can offer anything that you'd like to eat," Mr. Gray said as he showed her the living room and motioned for her to sit. "Casseroles coming out of my ears, but nothing to drink. Unless you like, uh, *tea*. I got a bottle, I mean a pot, of that."

An abundance of alcohol consumption could have explained the broken blood vessels in his face.

"I'm fine, Mr. Gray," Haley said, "but thank you."

"So, what's it you're wantin' to tell me."

Haley took a fortifying breath. Though she'd had to do it a multitude of times, she'd never gotten used to delivering bad news.

"What did the police tell you, Mr. Gray?" Haley asked.

"That she jumped."

"Do you believe them?"

Mr. Gray wrinkled his face. "I guess so. Why would they lie about something like that?"

"Did the news surprise you?" Haley said. "Was your wife showing signs of depression?"

"How the hell would I know? Who isn't depressed nowadays? And I don't get the meanin' of these questions."

They were interrupted by a thin elderly woman hunched over painfully in the shoulders. "*Jakob*," she said with a strong accent. "We have a visitor? You should've woken me up."

Mr. Gray huffed. "She sleeps as much as the kid."

The woman approached Haley and held out her hand. "I'm Jakob's mother, Mrs. Grabodski."

She glanced at Jacob Gray with a note of disapproval. "My Jakob is ashamed of being Polish. Says his name's Gray as if he could fool anyone that he's an Englishman."

"Mama!"

"Vat? It's true, no?"

Mr. Gray flicked his fingers. "Go make us some tea."

"Only the real kind. Not that nasty stuff that

makes you more wretched than you even are." She stared at Haley. "Poor Olivia. God rest her soul."

When Mrs. Grabodski left the room, Haley turned back to Mr. Gray.

"Did your wife come with you to Boston?"

"No, we met here. She'd left England after the war, to escape bad memories, she said. I was working then. Things were booming in the twenties. Now," he pounded his fist on the side table, and Haley startled. "It's nothin'! Unemployment is at an all time high and an honest man can't get a decent job. It's all for nothin'!"

Haley kept her expression bland. Mr. Gray wasn't beyond using physical force. Had the bruising on Mrs. Gray's arms been inflicted by him? Haley had known of husbands guilty of worse.

Mrs. Grabodski shuffled into the room with a tray of tea, and Haley stared at her as if she was willing the frail woman not to drop it. She expected Mr. Gray to help, but he simply sat there, waiting.

"Can I help you, Mrs. Grabodski?"

"I've got it, dear."

Haley didn't relax until Mrs. Grabodski safely delivered the tea to the coffee table.

Mrs. Grabodski poured for Haley. "Milk and sugar?"

"Yes, please."

Before she could pour for her son, Mr. Gray shifted sideways and pulled himself to his feet. "You don't mind if I have a cup of the *other kind of tea*, do you?" He limped into the kitchen without waiting for an answer.

"You must forgive my son," Mrs. Grabodski said. "He's had a hard life."

Haley sipped her tea, then said, "He must miss his wife terribly."

"*Ack*." Mrs. Grabodski shrugged her bony shoulder. "It wasn't like they were Romeo and Juliet."

"It's not uncommon for the feelings of love to wane after a long marriage." Haley took a risk that the lonely woman wouldn't be offended by a little probing.

Mrs. Grabodski set her teacup down, her hand trembling slightly. "Jakob and Olivia weren't a good match. I told him so from the beginning. He should marry a Polish woman, I told him. But no, he has to marry an English girl. And a widow, to boot. I wanted for my boy to have a fresh virgin."

Haley nearly choked on her tea. If Mrs. Grabodski were of a stronger constitution, she'd have jumped to the top of Haley's list of suspects.

"But at least she gave me a grandson," Mrs. Grabodski, added. "Only one, but *ack*, you can't force nature. Especially when the wife finds her comfort elsewhere."

"Are you saying that Mrs. Gray was having an affair?"

"*Ack.*"

Mr. Gray returned before his mother could say more. A little boy about the age of five held on to his empty arm as if it would save his life. "Don't mind this little feller," he said, dragging the child into the room with him. "Got strange when his mother—"

"It's fine," Haley replied. To the little boy, she said, "What's your name?"

Mr. Gray settled into the armchair with a heavy sigh. His young son, forced to release his father's arm, hid behind the chair. Haley smiled warmly when the boy's eyes, wide as saucers, peeked out from around the edge. Poor thing. It was never easy losing a parent, no matter your age—Haley had lost both of hers when she was in her thirties—but for this young boy, now without a mother because of a heinous crime, it was doubly sad.

"He stopped talking," Mrs. Grabodski said.

"I'm not sure what to tell you, Miss Higgins."

Haley ignored the demoted title. She opened the box of doughnuts and offered them to the boy. "Sugar doughnuts. Do you want one?"

The temptation was too much for the boy. He sprang out from behind the chair, grabbed a doughnut and, in a flash, returned to his hiding spot.

"Say thank you, you little rat!"

Haley's eyes widened in shock and disapproval at Mr. Gray's outburst. His temperament was proving to be unpredictable and volatile. *The kind of man who, after drinking a bottle of bootlegged whiskey, would kill his wife in a fit a passion?* Haley could picture him taking the stairs, even if it was seven flights on his bad leg, pulling the alarm, and in a fit of jealousy pushing his wife out the window.

If Mr. Gray sensed Haley's discomfort, he didn't show it. He grabbed a doughnut for himself and stuffed half of it into his mouth.

Haley pushed the box toward his mother.

"Mrs. Grabodski?"

"I don't mind if I do."

With the Gray/Grabodski family busily eating, Haley took a moment to take in the apartment. It was cluttered and dusty—the results of weeks of neglect, not merely the two days Mrs. Gray had been gone.

"Did Mrs. Gray like working at the Custom House?"

Mr. Gray wiped his mouth with the back of his sleeve. "She didn't talk about work much. Just how tired she was and didn't want to cook dinner. She harped on that, I tell you."

His wife worked all day and then was expected to

cook at the end of it too? Haley pressed. "Is there something you like to do to keep busy?"

"If I do, it ain't no concern of yours, see?" Mr. Gray slurped back the rest of his "tea," let out a belch, and then stood to his feet. "But if it's an alibi you're trying to get at, I was with my mother and my kid all day and all night long."

The boy stood in full view, but with this bellow from his father, he ducked out of sight again. "Now, I'm sure a workin' gal like yourself can find your way out." Then to his son, "Anthony!"

The timid child ran after him.

Mrs. Grabodski made to stand up, but Haley put a hand on her arm to stop her.

"It's okay, Mrs. Grabodski. Your son is right. I can find my way out."

Haley paused in the hallway and took a moment to muse. If she were married to that man, she'd be tempted to jump herself. *The question was, had he been in the building on the day Olivia Gray died? Had anyone seen him there?*

9

Samantha should've known that Haley wasn't kidding when she said she'd spy on her date with Richard Wentworth. What amused Samantha was that Haley hadn't come alone, but was accompanied by a gentleman friend. Wasn't she just full of surprises!

She and Haley were both very good, Samantha thought, at pretending not to know each other. Despite their tables being rather close together, neither showed more than a normal cursory interest in the other.

Mr. Wentworth pulled out a chair for Samantha, and she thanked him as she shifted closer to the table.

"I hope you don't mind my saying," her date said, "but you look ravishing."

The compliment pleased Samantha. The time she'd spent adding lace trim to lengthen her dress to make it more stylish had been worth the trouble, especially since he looked dapper in a cream-colored cotton suit.

He'd parted his dark hair on the side and combed it over and away from his forehead. Fine lines were etched around his eyes and mouth and scribbled in rows along his forehead, though it didn't take away from his good looks. If anything, it made him look distinguished—a person who smiled and frowned and spent time in deep contemplation. Samantha wouldn't doubt there was an interesting story behind those lines. Perhaps a story would come from their time spent together.

"Thank you, Mr. Wentworth."

"Please, call me Rick."

"And you must call me, Samantha."

"Samantha."

His tone caused Samantha to feel cherished, and she felt herself blush.

Rick went on. "Such a beautiful name."

The waiter came, and they ordered. Samantha glimpsed over at Haley who winked subtly. Haley's companion spoke quite animatedly about hospital drama. Haley smiled at the man and when she spoke she called him Gerald.

The roast beef and potato meal was scrumptious though it was a shame to pair it with apple juice.

Samantha hadn't eaten so well in ages; she almost forgot she was supposed to be on the job.

"Tell me about yourself," Rick said. "By your accent, I'd say you're local."

"Born and raised."

"Have you always wanted to be a reporter?"

Samantha patted her mouth with a napkin. "The job fell in my lap. I started as a receptionist at the paper. The reporting world grew on me, and one day, I knew I wanted to be a bigger part of it."

"So, you just went after it and took it," Rick said, blue eyes gleaming. "I admire that in a lady."

"I admire it in a *person*," Samantha said, then added. "And thank you."

Rick chuckled. "You're one those feminist reformers, aren't you?"

"And if I am?"

He grinned, and his charm oozed. "I've no problem with it."

Samantha caught sight of Haley giving a quick nod toward Mr. Wentworth. Right—she needed to be asking the questions!

"So, tell me, Rick, how long have you worked at the Custom House?"

"Only two weeks. I immigrated to America from London after the war, but I've only been back in Boston for a little while."

"You said you knew Olivia Gray by reputation, but did you ever have a chance to meet her? Maybe in passing?"

Rick chuckled. "Are you investigating me?"

Samantha felt her cheeks redden. *As subtle as a sledgehammer on brick*, she thought. She glanced at Haley who kept her gaze on her date, but Samantha didn't miss the twitch at the corner of her mouth.

"No. I'm just curious. It's the nature of my business, I suppose." She smiled with a slight incline of her head. Rick wasn't the only one who could pour on the charm. "And truthfully, if you knew something that would please my boss, I would be grateful."

He humored her by making a show of rubbing his chin in thought. "Let me see. From what I saw of Mrs. Gray, which wasn't much, she was pretty quick to speak her mind."

Samantha understood the need to speak up for oneself. "You have to be when you're a woman working amongst men."

Rick blinked, then smiled. "Yes, well, Mrs. Gray, from what I witnessed, had no problem speaking up for herself. She had a particular problem with Mr. Tapper, or rather, he had a problem with her."

"Why's that?"

"Rumor has it that she was up for promotion even though he had seniority. He filed a formal complaint stating that Mrs. Gray didn't deserve the promotion because she was married. That's the rumor, anyway."

Samantha couldn't stop herself from coming to the woman's defense. "Married women have responsibilities too."

"That's what husbands are for."

"Some husbands don't seem to know that."

"You talk as if you have some experience with husbands, Miss Hawke."

Oh dear. She *did* need to rein in her emotions!

"I'm closely acquainted with someone who does." She needed to take control and quickly changed the subject. "Do you miss England, Mr. Wentworth?"

"Rick, my dear. And not really. It's cold and damp and London's far too crowded for my taste. Boston has the charm of England but with more modern conveniences."

"I've never been abroad," Samantha said. "I've only ventured out of state as far as New York City."

"Oh, you simply must travel! There's no experience like it to broaden one's horizons. To experience with your senses the many cultures of the world."

Samantha thought of Talia and Bina and sighed inwardly. She'd just have to accept that her only experiences traveling abroad would be through the pages of a book. "I'll have to live vicariously through you, Rick."

His eyes twinkled. "For now."

Such sauce!

"Tell me about the places you've been."

"Well, the war was a great tour guide. I spent time in France and Belgium, of course, all soldiers did, and then my regiment was sent to Italy. After the war, I had to see something that wasn't war-torn, so I spent time in India and other British colonies."

Samantha couldn't help but feel awed by the presence of this handsome, intelligent, and well-travelled man.

"What is your position at the Custom House?" she asked. He most certainly had to have an important government spot.

He flicked a smooth palm. "It's boring, really. Endless chatting on the telephone and pushing papers. Now *your* job sounds interesting. What is the most exciting story you've ever written?"

Besides the one she hoped to write about Olivia Gray? If he could be coy, she could be too. She batted her eyelashes. "If you read the papers, Mr. Wentworth, you'd know."

"I do read the papers, Sam Hawke." His playful expression grew ominously serious. "It appears your job can become dangerous when you entwine yourself in other people's dirty laundry."

10

Haley couldn't help but shoot a look at Samantha after Richard Wentworth's last remark. He was an interesting man, and Haley couldn't quite put her finger on what both attracted her and cautioned her about him. He was flirty with Samantha, and his eyes sparkled in a way that indicated he was merely teasing her. He was a shameless ladies' man, the kind Haley had little patience with. She wouldn't be surprised if he "ran" into pretty girls and asked them to dinner on a regular schedule. Yet, something about him cautioned her.

Her date commanded her attention. "You seem a little distracted."

Dr. Gerald Mitchell, a delightful man, made an excellent doctor of geriatrics. He liked to joke that he was soon to be as old as his patients. In perfect health and mentally sharp, Haley considered him a good friend and an amusing companion. Gerald's wife, Elsa, was a stroke victim and an invalid who needed day and night nursing. Faithful to his wife, Gerald had never acted in an unseemly or disloyal way toward Haley. He disliked going to events alone, and they always enjoyed spirited conversations. It was an equitable relationship since Haley didn't consider herself the romantic type and was too busy for such frivolous engagements as the flirting she was witnessing at the table kitty-corner from her.

She gave Samantha credit. It would be difficult not to melt under those piercing blue eyes. Haley just hoped Samantha could last the luncheon without agreeing to a second date.

"I think I recognize that man," she said. "Do you know him?"

Gerald looked over his shoulder. "Isn't the lady a friend of yours?"

"Yes."

"Did you have an argument or something? You're acting as if you are strangers."

Haley decided now was a good time to confess to her subterfuge. "We're actually on a case; that man is a suspect."

Gerald stared. "Have you joined the police force now?"

"You know I work closely with the police."

"As a consultant. I didn't think you did reconnaissance missions."

"Fine, you caught me. I'm working a little on my own time."

"Dr. Higgins! *Again*? After what happened last time—"

Haley cut him off with a stern look and a finger to her lips. "Please, lower your voice."

Gerald, looking none too happy, complied. In a near whisper, he continued, "I would've thought you'd learned your lesson. Amateur sleuthing is a dangerous hobby."

Haley couldn't deny Gerald's accusation. She and Samantha had come close to dying on their last case.

Haley dropped her napkin on the table. "I'm sorry. I should've been more transparent when I invited you." She would've come alone, but that would've looked odd, and she hadn't wanted to risk attracting Richard Wentworth's attention.

"I'm glad you did. It's not like you're in any immediate danger anyway." He sighed. "What is it that you're working on?"

Haley held back a smile. While Gerald showed his displeasure at her "hobby," he always seemed fascinated to know the facts.

"My autopsy findings on the body of our victim suggest someone pushed her."

"I see. And how is this debonair gentleman involved?" A scandalous thought flashed behind his eyes. "Surely, he's not her husband?"

"No, Mr. Wentworth is a coworker. Samantha's fishing for information on what might be going on behind the scenes in Mrs. Gray's office. Her husband is our prime suspect. It appears his wife may have been having an affair, which is motive, and his alibi is thin. He's counting on the word of his timid five-year-old son and a frail elderly mother who would say anything to protect him."

"I see. And what does Detective Cluney make of things?"

Haley frowned at her friend. "We haven't yet had a chance to discuss the case together."

Gerald clucked. "I hope you'll find time to do so soon."

Haley was about to offer her reassurances when a young man with a confident swagger approached Samantha's table. She recognized him from the *Boston Daily Record*. Mr. Johnny Milwaukee.

"Samantha, doll!" he said brazenly. "And here you told me you weren't dating!"

Haley couldn't believe their bad luck. And poor Samantha looked like she could spit needles.

"What I do with my free time is my own business, Johnny."

Johnny Milwaukee extended a hand to Richard Wentworth who looked like he'd rather wrestle a snake than shake hands.

"Johnny Milwaukee."

"Richard Wentworth."

Johnny grinned at Samantha. "Sam and I went on a date once, didn't we doll?"

"Johnny!"

Richard stood to his feet and towered over Johnny by two inches. Haley worried they might have to intercept a brawl.

"If you don't mind, Mr. Milwaukee, the lady and I . . ."

"Sure thing, pal. Keep your shirt on. I'll leave the two of you to get cozy." He raised a hand and called to a man waiting at a table at the back of the room.

"Friend of yours?" Mr. Wentworth said to Samantha as he returned to his seat.

"Hardly. We work together. He can be such an imbecile."

When Richard Wentworth called for the check, Haley nodded for Gerald to do the same. When she and Gerald parted ways, she started her DeSoto and got it on the road in time to follow Samantha home.

Samantha had wisely said her goodbyes to her date before waving down a taxi.

Haley thought she'd stop to chat with Samantha when she arrived at the offices of the *Boston Daily Record* so they could compare notes, but the taxi carried on past there, until it stopped on the street in front of a run-down tenement building.

Haley remained in her car when Samantha got out of the cab. *Did she have a new lead*? Haley couldn't think of anything she'd heard Wentworth say that would've led Samantha here. When Samantha disappeared inside, Haley followed.

The names of the tenants were listed by the door. Haley eyed the list and one name popped out at her: Rosenbaum.

This was where Samantha lived? Now Haley understood why Samantha wanted no one to know.

Haley returned to her DeSoto and headed back to the morgue.

11

Haley had been expecting the call when it came. Detective Cluney had sounded more than just a little perturbed when he'd requested she come to the station to meet with him.

She found him ensconced behind his large desk that looked smaller due to the clutter covering every square inch. They had a tenuous working relationship. He'd rather have worked with a man than a woman, but a woman trumped an Englishman. He gave her allowances he wouldn't give to others because she was assistant chief medical examiner—and truthfully, everyone knew Haley was less of the assistant than Dr. Guthrie was—and he needed her cooperation.

His barely contained frustration was evident by the redness gathered around his neck.

"Dr. Higgins. Let's get right to brass tacks. I hear

you're investigating my case, which I'm closing, by the way."

"I've determined Mrs. Gray's death isn't suicide as we first thought. I sent you my report."

Detective Cluney picked up a green file folder and slapped it down again. "I got it. An unauthorized autopsy. Does the mayor know?"

"I performed it on my own time."

"Without permission from the next of kin. Do you know how much trouble we could get into if the husband files a complaint?"

"Yes, but the results suggest someone murdered Mrs. Gray, and her husband is on the top of the suspect list."

"*Whose* suspect list, Dr. Higgins? Clearly not mine!"

"I understand why you are upset—"

"Of course, I'm upset! You're usurping my authority."

"I only made private enquiries to support my conclusions before coming to you, so as not to waste your time."

"But you *are* wasting my time, Dr. Higgins. Mr. Gray called here, you know, telling us to keep you from coming back to his home."

Haley felt the weight of defeat. "I brought doughnuts. And my condolences."

Detective Cluney shook his head and clucked his tongue. He removed a cigar from a desk drawer, clipped the end, and lit it. After releasing a puff of gray smoke, he made a show of opening the file. "You've decided it wasn't suicide based on the area of impact and the way the bones were broken. The fall was from the seventh floor. Surely, there's no way to tell how her body would spin through the air before hitting the ground."

"It was a theory at first, but then I performed an experiment." Haley relayed how she and Thomas Martin had built the dummy and dropped it from Olivia Gray's office window.

To Haley's deep dismay, Detective Cluney broke out in a hearty laugh. "That is the craziest darned thing I've ever heard. You expect that to stand up in a court of law?"

Haley jutted her chin out. She hated not being taken seriously. "Detective Cluney, please. Take a step back from my unorthodox methods for one moment. A woman has died. There is reason to believe she may not have jumped. Isn't that enough to warrant further investigation? Aren't you in the least bit curious as to what I've discovered through my inquiries?"

Detective Cluney tapped ash into the tray. "Very well. Let me hear it."

"Besides the experiment with the dummy, Mrs.

Gray had many skin cells under the fingers of one hand. Plus, fresh scratches on the back of her hands could be a sign of a struggle."

"Or she was just itchy and clumsy."

Haley ignored his ignorance and pushed on. "As you know, I paid a visit to Mr. Gray. It's my opinion, despite prohibition, he suffers from alcoholism. He imbibed while I was there, in the middle of the day, and enlarged capillaries covered his nose."

"So, that doesn't make him a killer."

"I met his mother, Mrs. Grabodski—Gray is the Anglicized version of his birth name—and she confided that she didn't like Olivia Gray and blamed her for her son's unhappiness."

"Doesn't mean he climbed the tower and pushed her out of the window."

"No, but it does give him a motive."

Detective Cluney shrugged a shoulder in begrudging assent.

"It also turns out one of the people sharing office space with Mrs. Gray, a Mr. Tapper, had a well-known objection to having a married woman employed. Apparently, she was in line for a promotion he thought he deserved. It might be worth looking at him."

Detective Cluney narrowed thoughtful eyes. "How do you know this?"

Haley wasn't about to admit she'd spent the

previous lunchtime eavesdropping on Samantha's date. "I can't say at the moment, but I believe the source to be reliable."

"Can't say? Source? Are you a pathologist or a bloody journalist now?"

"I'm sorry. This person wouldn't appreciate my bringing his name up in an unofficial interview." Haley was loath to bring up another unsavory motive when she didn't have more proof, but with a murder involved, she felt it prudent to bring the possibility to the detective's attention. "It's been hinted at that Mrs. Gray may have been having an affair with one of the men in her office."

"Your source again?"

Haley simply smiled.

"Fine." Detective Cluney stubbed out his cigar. "I'll have my guys ask around. Maybe there are more talkers at the Custom House, someone who may have seen Mr. Gray lurking about, or knows something about the office politics."

"That's all I ask."

"Yah, yah. I suppose it's too much for me to ask that you leave police business to the police."

Haley recognized she was being dismissed and stood. She smiled slyly. "Of course, Detective."

He guffawed behind her as she walked away, both

of them knowing better. Haley had no intention of butting out.

Molly had a roasted chicken ready and on the table by the time Haley got home.

Mr. Midnight hopped-hobbled on his three legs, took a moment to rub against Haley's pant leg, and indulged in slivers of chicken that Molly had added to his dish.

"You spoil him, Molly."

"What? A little chicken is nothing."

The radio played in the background with the melodious tones of Kate Smith singing "*Dream a Little Dream of Me.*"

Molly led them in a prayer of thanks then asked, "How was your day?"

Haley chewed as she considered the question. "I've convinced Detective Cluney that Jacob Gray is a viable suspect for the murder of his wife."

Haley relayed her awkward conversation with Detective Cluney.

"To be fair, though," Haley went on, "he does have a good argument. Interrogating suspects and witnesses is out of my jurisdiction. But he was ready to close the case, and I'm nearly a hundred percent sure I'm right about it being murder."

Nearly sure.

"It doesn't sound to me like this Jacob Gray and Olivia Gray were a good match to begin with," Molly said.

"I heartily agree. From all accounts, Olivia was a resourceful, intelligent, and attractive woman. Jacob is bitter and unkind." She thought about the bruising on Olivia's wrists. "I'm afraid he'd been manhandling his wife."

"Perhaps he wasn't always that way," Molly said. "This depression affects people in different ways. Some men simply lose who they are if they're not working. I can imagine it was hard for him to take that his wife had become the breadwinner of the family."

Haley admired Molly's intuitiveness.

"It wouldn't be the first time a woman thought she was marrying one kind of man and ended up being married to another kind all together." Haley couldn't help but think of Samantha's experience with Seth Rosenbaum.

They finished eating, and Molly began the cleanup. "I can take care of this," she said. "There's a pitcher of iced tea in the refrigerator. It'll help to cool you down. I heard on the radio that it went up to a hundred and nine degrees in Florida today. Can you imagine?"

12

After her lunch with Rick Wentworth, Samantha went home to change back into her work suit. She didn't want to draw attention by returning to work in a fancy dress she hadn't been wearing that morning.

Johnny Milwaukee sat casually at his desk, smoking a cigarette, and unabashedly staring at her. Samantha fumed. He even had the audacity to wink!

Though they both had clearance from Mr. August to sniff out a story on company time, she had to continue to fill her original assignments to write the daily women's columns. While Johnny shot the breeze, drank coffee, smoked, and jawed on about the latest ball game with the equally arrogant Freddy Hall, she wrote about how to keep a soufflé from collapsing.

Soufflés have a reputation for being temperamental, but they're very simple—

"Sorry to interrupt, doll."

Samantha snorted. "What do you want, Johnny? Can't you see that one of us is working?"

"Hey, I'm working." He pointed a finger to his head. "It's all business up here, doll."

"Well, go away."

"I wondered if you wanted to go on another date? Or is that grifter your main squeeze now?"

"I'm no one's main squeeze, and he's not a grifter—he has a respectable job—and you and I never went on a *first* date."

"Ow, that hurt. Well then, why not make our next date our first date?"

Johnny was insufferable. What he lacked in Hollywood good looks, he made up with charm in spades. Samantha couldn't help feeling attracted—she was a young maybe-widow after all. But she'd never give the wise guy any satisfaction.

"No. And don't try to tell me I'll get a lead for a story if I do."

"You might," Johnny said with a smirk. "And I'm not just saying that."

Samantha narrowed her eyes suspiciously. "Don't play with me, Johnny." Her coworker knew how important this job was to her—she needed the money to support her daughter and mother-in-law, and Mr. August had thrown a nice bonus her way last time she worked a big case. Johnny also knew about the rush and what it did for your ego. Did he see that need in her? To have her feathers stroked.

Drat that man!

Samantha focused her gaze on the sheet of paper moving through the typewriter as she typed. "You'll have to give me more than a thin promise, Johnny."

He chuckled then returned to his seat throwing a verbal teaser over his shoulders. "Not everything is on the square, doll."

What did he mean by that? Samantha refused to give Johnny the satisfaction of knowing he'd piqued her curiosity. Besides, she knew more than Johnny did about the Gray case. He certainly couldn't know about Haley's autopsy report and her experiment with the dummy. So, he couldn't be referring to that.

Then what?

Oh, that man!

Finally, the day ended, and Samantha gathered her things. She offered a general "good night" to the room and began her trek home.

Johnny pulled up beside her in his roadster.

"Wanna ride, doll?"

The heat felt smothering, and truth be told, her exhaustion overwhelmed her. She'd love a ride! But she couldn't bear having Johnny Milwaukee discover that she lived in the tenements.

She kept walking. "No, thanks."

The roadster glided slowly beside her. "Now, come on. Don't be sore. It's all part of the job, right? Keeping leads close to the chest. What d'ya say, Sam? I'll show you mine if you show me yours."

"Now, you shut your filthy trap, Mr. Milwaukee. I may be a competitor, but I'm still a lady."

Johnny pulled over, stopped the car, and jumped out. He had the decency to look contrite.

"You're right. I'm sorry." He walked backward in front of her, ducking to catch her eyes.

"Out of my way, Johnny."

"Not until you accept my apology."

"Fine, I accept. Now go."

"All right. But don't stay mad at me, Sam. We have more in common than you think."

Johnny strolled back to his car and made a U-turn. Samantha didn't turn the corner onto Stillman Street until she was sure he was out of sight and couldn't possibly see which direction she was headed.

The ache in her sore back and feet seemed to lessen when Samantha's head began to throb. She really needed to put her feet up and sip on a glass of good Canadian whiskey. She'd have to wait to do the first, and imagine the second. Dragging herself up the steps, the smell of old grease only made her headache worse. The O'Connors were at it again. Samantha hoped Mrs. O'Connor wouldn't be sporting a new bruise in the morning.

"Home twice in one day," Bina said when Samantha stumbled in. "Home for another costume change?"

Samantha was too tired to fight. "Where's Talia?"

"She's having supper with a friend."

Samantha sat up straight. "What friend?"

"Your daughter has friends. You would know this if you spent more time at home. Why don't you go back to that receptionist job? At least you had regular hours."

"And less money."

"Money isn't everything."

"You wouldn't be saying that if we didn't have it."

Besides, the tediousness of the receptionist job had nearly driven Samantha crazy. Being a reporter was exciting. Every day was a different adventure.

But Bina was right about something. Money wasn't the most important thing.

"When does Talia get home?"

"I'm picking her up at seven."

"I'll pick her up."

"You don't know where the Abrams live."

Samantha's maternal guilt kicked into full gear. "Then you can draw me a map. I'm picking her up."

Dinner alone with Bina was too quiet, and quite honestly, a little depressing. Samantha left the table to turn on the radio, and they listened in peace to the Guy Lombardo Orchestra.

Her mind drifted, and she found herself thinking about her date with Richard Wentworth and what she'd learned about Mrs. Gray from him. She had enough information to go to Mr. August, but not enough to write a clean story.

If she took in what she knew, Mr. August might demand she write a tabloid piece. Scandals sold papers. Even if it meant running a follow-up story to set the facts straight, the editor didn't care. It would mean running Mr. Gray up the flag pole, but what if he wasn't guilty? She hadn't had a chance to look under the lids of Mrs. Gray's office coworkers. There could be a lot of dirt there.

Samantha couldn't do a sloppy job. Haley Higgins would never trust her again, and besides that, it just didn't feel right. Mr. August might sack her if he ever discovered she'd had an inside scoop and hadn't brought it to him. She just had to make sure he didn't find out.

13

Samantha, by far the best typist in the room, couldn't help but feel a little smug as she watched the others peck away at their typewriters with two fingers. Rays of morning sunshine beat through the windows. At one time, a resourceful newsman had taped old newspaper—now faded to almost clear—along the top panes of glass. A loud din of low male voices, murmured telephone calls, typewriter bells, and the chatter of telegram machines filled the space—such a common sound to Samantha, she barely registered the noise.

Johnny lit a cigarette then shouted over the cacophony. "What are you working on, Sam? July fourth picnic ideas?"

Samantha scowled. As it so happened, she was doing such a piece for the ladies' pages, but that wasn't what she was working on now. She'd finally let Mr. August in on what she'd learned about the Gray case, and he'd told her to get something ready in case there was a break in the story. That break had come last night with the arrest of Jacob Gray.

But she wasn't about to leak her scoop. "What if I am? You might benefit from my efforts. Assuming that there's someone in your life who cooks and would invite you to join them."

"Ah, doll, I thought that would be you."

Samantha scoffed. "Not in a million years."

Johnny slapped his chest and feigned hurt. "I'm wounded."

Samantha decided to turn the tables. "What are you working on? Nothing? Again? I'm surprised Mr. August keeps you around."

"As it turns out, I'm on a story. Believe me, doll, when it breaks, it's gonna be big."

Samantha pursed her lips as she considered her coworker's boast. Was he pulling her leg, or was he onto something? He had been acting overly secretive lately.

"I don't believe you."

"What you believe don't change the truth. Hey Max!" Max had entered the room to collect folders ready to be filed. "Watch my desk, will ya? Nature calls." Before Max could protest, Johnny skipped out of the room as if his latest mug of coffee had just now made irresistible demands on his bladder.

Samantha's gaze met Max's then slid over to Johnny's desk. Johnny, in his haste, had carelessly left one of his files open. Was his "big story" recorded there? Samantha watched the other men in the room, all of whom didn't give a donkey's tail that Johnny had gone to use the restroom. Max had collected his files and left. Even Fred was out of the room. He was the only one who'd hassle her if he caught her snooping.

Not that she snooped, per se. She was simply walking by Johnny's empty desk on her way to the pencil sharpener mounted on the wall just beyond.

Despite Johnny's lackadaisical demeanor and somewhat sloppy style of dressing, he was meticulous in the way he kept his desk. On the wooden surface, wiped clean of dust, sat his shiny black typewriter and his coffee cup, rinsed and dried. A calendar with squares, filled with some kind of shorthand script, covered much of his desktop. Everyone in the newsroom carried about a certain amount of paranoia.

Which was why the open file on Johnny's desk was suspicious. Did he *want* her to see what was inside? He was certainly taking his time with the call of nature.

She glanced at the open folder, pushed away a twinge of guilt, and frowned. Several papers were facing printed-side down except for a small piece of notepaper scribbled with two German names: Frieder Ginsberg and Gerhardt Sommerfeld.

Samantha heard Johnny whistling as he came down the hall. She scooted to the pencil sharpener and briskly turned the crank on an already sharpened pencil. She blew on the lead and sauntered past Johnny to her desk. She focused hard on the paper in her typewriter, but the words just blurred before her. She couldn't help but cast a curious glance Johnny's way.

He grinned knowingly.

Drat that man! He knew she'd snooped. But the bigger question? Why had he wanted her to peek? What was it about those two names, and why did he want her to see them?

Samantha refused to acknowledge Johnny. Let him think she hadn't taken the bait. She focused on the story about Olivia and Jacob Gray then read it over once before making a show of releasing it from the typewriter carriage. She headed for the editor's office.

When Samantha returned to the pit, Johnny was gone along with the file. *Where had he gone? And what was the deal about those names?*

It wasn't like she could track down Johnny. He had a car, and she only had her two good legs.

German names. Were they men who'd immigrated

to Boston after the Great War? What was Johnny's interest in them?

Sighing, she put a clean sheet of paper into her typewriter. Economical Treats for Independence Day Celebration, she typed. The *Boston Daily Record* subscribed to several ladies' magazines for Samantha's benefit, and she thumbed through the latest editions. It wasn't a problem for her to draw from another source if she gave proper attribution, but it would be nice to have something original. She wondered if Bina had a personal recipe she'd be willing to share.

Knowing how Bina took pride in her baking, it was not likely, but it never hurt to ask. The perceived glamor of having her name in print might entice her. Just think, she'd be the envy of her friends! Samantha could imagine the tug of war as Bina adamantly declined and then begrudgingly, but secretly wanting to, gave in. Samantha would let her have that win if she scooped the recipe.

At any rate, she had the lead story on the Gray case, and she felt pleased with that.

14

One perk of working for a newspaper was a trip to the library for research could be viewed as a perfectly legitimate way to spend time out of the office.

The Boston Public Library, an impressive stone building on the corner of Boylston and Dartmouth Street in the Back Bay area, was too far a walk for Samantha. She waved down a taxi, with every intention of submitting the receipt to Mr. August for reimbursement. On the ride over, she held her hat with one hand and pushed stray strands of hair behind her ear with the other. Messy hair was the price of taking a vehicle in the summer with the window open wide.

Her thoughts drifted to an earlier discussion with Haley about the unhappy marriage of Jacob and Olivia Gray. *What had initiated that marriage? Had they once been in love? Or had Olivia Gray found herself in the family way, like I did? Was that why she'd married such a beast of a man?*

For all Seth's faults, at least Samantha could say he'd never laid a rough hand on her. No, her husband had been all charm and promises, with no backbone.

Had been? Samantha shocked herself at her use of the past tense. Did she *really* think Seth was dead? Maybe a part of her hoped so, if only because the idea he simply didn't care about her and his daughter, or his pain-in-the-neck mother, was a more painful option.

Maybe it was time just to face the facts. Seth was gone—*dead*—and wasn't ever coming back. The law was on her side. But what would that mean for them, if she made an official declaration? Having a son, husband, or father who abandoned his family garnered pity—having one who died garnered sympathy.

And not to be made light of, once she made a legal statement regarding Seth's death, she would be free to date again, even marry, though she couldn't imagine any man who'd be willing to take on Bina. And even if she were no longer legally bound to care for her dead husband's widowed mother, she felt morally bound.

The taxi let Samantha out at the front entrance. She paid the driver, insisted on a receipt, and once inside the library, searched for her old friend Patty Kingston, who worked in the newspaper reading room.

It was an unlikely place for Patty to work as she loved to chat and gossip. A remnant of the flapper girls from more prosperous times, Patty hung on to the glory days with a wardrobe of intricate boyish-cut dresses, hemmed too high for today's fashion.

Samantha waved across the whisper-quiet room filled with men catching up on continental and trans-continental news, and Patty blew her a kiss back.

They hugged, emitting quiet giggles as Patty dragged Samantha into a storage room and closed the door.

"Samantha, darling! How good to see you! I haven't seen you in ages!"

"I've been busy."

"I know! I saw your byline in the paper! I boasted about you like crazy, 'That's my friend! She's playing with the big boys!' Oh my, that's right; you were almost killed!"

"Well, I wasn't killed. In fact, I wasn't even injured."

"Oh, but the danger was there! So exciting. My life's been such a bore with this ridiculous prohibition. Thank goodness for the clubs, or I'd perish for sure."

Samantha couldn't help but smile at her boisterous friend.

"How's work?"

"Dreadfully boring. But with the depression on,

Daddy cut off my allowance. It costs money to have fun, ya know."

Patty's hair was cut in a short bob, and she fingered the curls. "I'd die for a cigarette right now. That's one of the many things I hate about this job. No smoking in the library. No smoking outside for women." Her voice pitched upwards as she mimicked. "'Smoking is unseemly for the gentler sex and not something we want the library to be associated with.'"

Samantha burst out laughing, then cupped a hand over her mouth. "The things we put up with just to get a paycheck."

Patty snorted. "It could be worse. So, how's that sweet daughter of yours?"

"She's in school now."

"No! *Really*? Where has the time gone?" She wrinkled her nose. "And *Bina*?"

Patty and Bina were like oil and water, and neither saw any good in the other.

"She's still Bina. She helps me with Talia while I work. I'm thankful for that."

"Which brings me to Seth. Any word?"

Samantha shook her head.

"Such a snake. Sorry, darling, but that's the truth." Patty opened the storage a crack and peeked out. "Drat. I have to get back to the desk, in case they need me."

"Well, I need you."

"I knew you weren't here just because you missed me."

"But I do miss you, Patty."

Patty stroked Samantha's arm. "I know you do, darling. Tell me what you're looking for."

Samantha followed Patty to the desk where she kept her voice low and asked for help to find anything mentioning the word *Iserlohn*. Johnny's interest in her German-made pen with the same name had made her curious. Johnny had seen that pen before, often, but only now did the name of it jump out at him. Now that he carried about a note with two German names.

"Lucky for you, darling, cross-referencing is what I do."

Patty went to a wall of card files and opened a drawer under the letter *I*.

"How do you spell that again?"

"I-S-E-R-L-O-H-N. It's pronounced *Esserloan*."

"Here's the reference card." Patty removed it from the file drawer and handed it to Samantha.

"These are the stories recorded about that ship, paper name, date, and page number. Would you like me to pull the editions for you?"

"If you don't mind."

"I don't mind. It helps to pass the time."

Patty produced the papers and left Samantha

alone at one of the tables to read them. Some articles were about the pens themselves, a quality pen made by Brause, a company out of Westfalen, Germany. It boasted a handy plunger apparatus. The user was to dip the nib into an inkwell and turn the screw at the other end to suck the ink into the barrel. Samantha hadn't realized, until that moment, how special the pen from her late father-in-law was.

The New York Times proved the most interesting. According to its reporter, the merchant cargo ship that arrived in New York from Germany was called the SS *Iserlohn*. The British were known to set up blockades to sink the ships. The United States of America was still neutral in the war, but Woodrow Wilson had decided to keep the German ships in port against their will. He stated that action was to protect the German sailors. Whatever the former president's real reasons for detaining the sailors were, the public wasn't happy about his decision.

Samantha stared blankly in front of her. Was this the story that Johnny was after? But why? And why now?

Time spent playing golf was the only time Haley's mind was ever off her job. Long walks on the greens, strategic golf shots, and clean air offered the break she needed. Besides the Gray case, the morgue was experiencing a lull. Nothing was happening that Mr. Martin and Dr. Guthrie couldn't handle.

Haley had played a good game and was now driving home from the golf club in Brookline. She twisted the knob of her Motorola—thankful she'd convinced herself to splurge on the car radio—and Calloway & His Cotton Club Orchestra resounded with their top hit song, "*Minnie the Moocher*." She soon found herself singing along.

"Folks, here's a story 'bout Minnie the Moocher

SHE WAS *a red-hot hoochie-coocher*
She was the roughest, toughest frail
But Minnie had a heart as big as a whale.

Hi-dee hi-dee hi-dee hi (hi-dee hi-dee hi-dee hi)

WHOA-A-A-A-AH (WHOA-A-A-A-AH)

Hee-dee-hee-dee-hee-dee-hee (hee-dee-hee-dee-hee-dee-hee)

He-e-e-e-e-e-e-y (he-e-e-e-e-e-e-y)"

. . .

When Haley finally drove up to her Grove Street apartment, she spotted Molly disappearing into the building. Odd, Haley thought. Not that Molly had gone out, but that she'd quite clearly pretended not to see Haley when Haley was most certain she had. Molly practically ran inside.

Haley caught up to her housekeeper before she got to the top floor. The stairs were a good exercise for both, but Haley was younger and fitter.

"Hello, Molly," she said as they entered the apartment together.

"Oh, hello, Dr. Higgins. I didn't see you there."

Molly's face flushed a rosy red, but somehow Haley doubted it was solely from the rapid climb.

"Is everything all right?" Haley asked as they each removed their hats and gloves and set them on the rack by the door.

"Yes, why wouldn't it be?" Molly hurried to the kitchen; Haley propped her clubs against the wall and followed.

Haley persisted. It wasn't like Molly to keep secrets from her. "You seem flustered about something. Maybe I can help."

Molly carefully pulled an apron over her neatly

styled and pinned hair. "It's nothing. I only had a coffee with a friend."

"Oh, who?" Haley knew Molly's friends as most were mutual.

Molly let out a breath. "I might as well tell you since you're bound to find out anyway. Not that it means anything."

Haley's stomach clenched in worry. Was coffee with a friend a euphemism for an appointment with a doctor? She did hope nothing serious was wrong. "What is it?"

"I had breakfast with Dr. Guthrie."

"What?" Haley had braced herself for bad news, but surely if Molly needed the advice of a doctor, she'd go to her practitioner, not a pathologist. She would've come to Haley, herself.

"I don't understand."

"It's not that complicated, Dr. Higgins," she said with her chin in the air. "Dr. Guthrie called me yesterday and asked if I'd like to have breakfast with him at the Bell and Hand, not his home, and I said yes. I've just returned."

"You went on a date with Dr. Guthrie?" Haley heard the disbelief in her words. "I mean. That's . . . something. I'm just surprised."

"Why?" Molly's chin rose even higher. "Because a

distinguished gentleman such as Dr. Guthrie would be interested in the company of the likes of me?"

Molly's stance was defensive, and Haley thought this was the nearest they'd ever gotten to an argument.

"No. Of course not," she shot back. The Irish and the English were historically unfriendly, but Molly McPhail and Peter Guthrie were in America now and had more in common coming from the United Kingdom than not. And they were both single. "I think it's fantastic."

Molly's shoulders relaxed. "Do you really?"

Haley smiled though she thought it more frightful than fantastic. She had to live with one and work with the other, and if things ended badly, it was bound to be awkward all around But, if she wanted to defuse the tension, it was the appropriate thing to say.

"Yes."

Molly gushed like a schoolgirl. "He's such a gentleman, he is, and has a good sense of humor. We had quite a laugh."

Haley wondered if they could be talking about the same man. "Is that so?"

"He's rather impressed with you. Says you could run the place if they'd let you, only too bad you're a woman. I said that wouldn't matter one day, just wait and see."

Haley bit her lip to stifle a smile. "I'm going to clean up a little."

"You do that, and I'll have lunch on in a jiffy."

Before Haley put her clubs away, the telephone rang. As usual, Molly took the call. "Dr. Higgins' residence. Hello? What? Who's this?" She stared at the receiver and then back at Haley.

"What is it, Molly? Wrong number?"

"The caller didn't identify herself, but I believe it was a message for you."

"What did she say?"

"You got the wrong guy."

15

By the time Samantha made it to her apartment, she felt like she'd walked a marathon. The heat didn't help and neither did her new formfitting dress. She'd splurged on it with the bonus she'd gotten from her last big story, but she missed the loose-fitted style of the '20s. The only fan they owned was blowing, though it did little to take the edge off the heat.

Bina was in the kitchen entertaining the widow Mrs. Ginsberg, one of her close friends. She remained in the tenements because she couldn't afford to migrate to a more friendly and affluent part of Boston as many Jews had.

"You're home already?" Bina said, rising to her feet.

"It's almost five," Samantha replied. "Hello, Mrs. Ginsberg."

Mrs. Ginsberg had charcoal-gray hair pulled back in a tight, low bun. Her face was a map of wrinkles, especially around her wide mouth which was well exercised in gossip.

"Hello, Samantha. You look good. Have you put on a few pounds?"

Samantha couldn't imagine gaining weight with the walking she did and the lunches she skipped.

Mrs. Ginsberg didn't wait to hear her answer. "It used to be so much easier to put on a pound or two, before rationing. Not certain how anyone manages it."

Samantha simply nodded, then enquired politely about the woman's brother who lived on the same floor but at the other end of the hall.

"How's Mr. Falkner?"

"Oh, he's fine so long as he doesn't have to lift a finger to help me. He's too busy playing chess with his friend Gustav Schmidt at Copley Square. Gustav Schmidt is a hundred if he's a day. One day, I tell Georgie, you're going to show up, and he won't be there. Then who will you play your precious chess game with? Not me. Why? Because of all the years he refused to teach me, that's why. Not that I care for the game anyway."

Samantha smiled courteously, then turned to Bina. "Where's Talia?"

"In her room. She was tired after school; I think she's sick. I sent her to bed to sleep."

A shot of worry slid down Samantha's spine like a venomous snake, and she hurried to her daughter's room. "Talia?"

Talia sat cross-legged on the bed and played with a rag doll.

Samantha rushed to her daughter and placed a hand on her forehead.

"Bubba says you're not feeling well?"

"I'm okay. I just don't like Mrs. Ginsberg."

"Mrs. Ginsberg can be a lot to take, but you must respect your elders."

"I do respect her, Mommy. It's just easier to do when I'm in here."

Samantha smiled softly in relief. Her daughter was kind and had good sense to boot.

"Tell me about your new friend Sarah." Samantha was happy to learn that Talia had recently acquired a new friend."

"She's nice. I like her mommy." Talia hugged her doll tightly. "Why can't you stay at home with me? I'm tired of Bubba."

Samantha sighed and sat on the bed beside her sweet daughter.

"We've been through this, Talia."

"But all the kids' moms stay home. Why am I different?"

"Some mothers have to work." Samantha's mind went to Olivia Gray. "It's a hard time right now, and we all have to live with something we don't like. In our case, it's me having to go to work. But I'll tell you what. My next day off, we'll spend the whole day at the beach."

"Just you and me?"

Samantha mussed her daughter's blond head. "Just you and me, kiddo."

Bina and Mrs. Ginsberg now chatted at the door when Samantha came to see about helping with supper. Bina was usually more conscious of the time, but then the longer days with more sunlight made it easy to lose track.

". . . When we lost Frieder. Georgie says I should just put a headstone at his grave already—face facts—but I'm not giving up that Frieder might come home one day. I just can't think to put a gravestone on a plot of ground when there's no body to go with it. You understand that, don't you, Bina? With your Seth gone. . ."

Samantha left the two women to commiserate over their grief and headed to the kitchen to figure out what Bina intended to put together for supper. Lately, it was rye bread with cold cuts from the kosher market and cucumber salad. Samantha didn't mind a cold meal in this heat, but she tired of the same thing every night.

Beggars can't be choosers. She opened the ice box and pulled out the sandwich supplies. While washing the cucumbers, something niggled in the back of her mind.

Frieder Ginsberg.

The name of Mrs. Ginsberg's lost son. Also, one of the names on the list she'd found on Johnny's desk.

16

It'd been a while since Haley had met up with Samantha and she thought it was time they caught up and exchanged notes. So first thing the next morning, she drove to the newspaper building on Water Street and asked to see Miss Hawke.

The young receptionist disappeared and returned a minute later with Samantha on her heels.

"Dr. Higgins," Samantha said with a smile. "I was just thinking about you?"

"I have news you might be interested in." On seeing the nosy receptionist's furtive glances, she added, "Professionally."

"Let me get my things."

"I'm parked outside," Haley said. "I'll wait for you there."

Samantha joined her shortly and hopped in. "Where are we going?"

"To the Custom House."

Samantha shot her a look. "What for? I thought Mr. Gray was apprehended."

Haley started the engine, put the DeSoto into gear, and pulled into the flow of traffic.

"I got an anonymous telephone call yesterday. The caller said that we had the wrong man."

"Oh, no," Samantha said. "And my story about Jacob Gray went out today. Maybe it was a prank call. People are strange. They'll do anything for attention."

"True. Assuming this caller knows who the real killer is, why not go to the police?"

"Maybe she's afraid," Samantha said. "Don't forget I got a tip too."

"It wouldn't hurt to talk to a few people who knew Olivia Gray."

"I wonder what her colleagues thought of Jacob Gray."

"I can tell you I didn't think much of him." Haley relayed her awkward encounter with Mr. Gray and his mother.

"I can't help but wonder why a woman like Olivia Gray—intelligent, driven, attractive—would marry a man like that?"

"That's the million-dollar question."

Haley pulled into an empty spot and cut the engine. "I imagine the beginning of such an arrangement looks a lot rosier."

Samantha laughed humorlessly. "I can attest to that. Just listen to me—judging Olivia Gray when I'm guilty of the same thing."

Haley felt a wave of remorse. "Forgive me, that was insensitive."

Instead of responding to Haley's apology, she asked, "Why have you never married?"

Haley paused with the door half-opened.

"I'm sorry," Samantha said. "That's too personal."

"No, it's fine. I'm not opposed to the institution. My very good friend Ginger Reed is deliriously happy in her marriage, so I know it can be a rewarding arrangement. But I'd rather focus on my work. The single life is convenient for me."

They exited the car and fell into stride as they walked toward the Custom House.

"You don't miss romance?" Samantha asked. "I mean, for all intents and purposes, I've been living as a widow, but I confess, I miss having a man about, you know to keep you warm at night and *so forth.*" She smiled with a glint in her eyes. "Seth was good in that regard—when he was around."

"There have been gentlemen that have caught my interest," Haley admitted, "but then my brother was murdered, and I didn't have the time or the wherewithal to entertain thoughts about romance and marriage. It was more important to solve his case, and on failing that, to solve other cases. Like Mrs. Gray's."

Inside the Custom House, Haley and Samantha approached the receptionist together, but Samantha picked up her pace to get to the counter a second before Haley.

"I'm Samantha Hawke from the *Boston Daily Record*, and this is Dr. Higgins, the assistant chief medical examiner."

A man with a no-nonsense air about him, tugged on his suit vest and eyed Samantha up and down. His name tag was pinned over his right jacket pocket. Mr. Wallace.

"I don't see how I can help you."

"It's about the death of Mrs. Gray."

"I'm afraid I can't—"

"Mr. Wallace," Haley said cutting in. "I work closely with the police, and we are here in good faith with them. If you'd like to call Detective Cluney to verify, go ahead, we'll wait. He's a busy man, but I'm sure he won't mind."

Mr. Wallace's frown deepened. "Very well. As you probably know, her office is on the seventh floor. Mr. Snow can help you."

They entered the elevator and stood in silence as

the liftboy closed the metal gate. It was a slow climb. Haley leaned in close to Samantha and whispered, "Did you see any sign of Mr. Wentworth?"

Samantha shook her head. "Not so far, but I'm glad. I'd hate it if he thought I was here spying on him."

The bell dinged, and the doorman announced, "Seventh floor."

Having been to the office space before, Haley knew exactly how to get there. She reached a closed door and knocked. Soon after, a youthful man with ginger hair and a nervous stance opened the door. Once again, Haley made introductions.

"I'm Dr. Higgins with the coroner's office, and this is my colleague, Miss Hawke, from the *Boston Daily Record*. Mr. Wallace says that you can help us."

"I'm not sure how, but I'm happy to oblige."

Mr. Snow waved them inside but kept the door open. Haley strolled to the window.

"Nice views from the tower," she said. "It must be like a moving picture, different every day."

"It is, it is. And with every season. It can be quite breathtaking on some days."

"Do you like working here?" Samantha asked. "I'm thinking of making a move out of journalism, but I don't know."

"Are you good with facts and figures?" Mr. Snow asked. "Numbers and the like?"

Samantha circled the office making hemming and hawing noises. "I'm more of a visual person, I think."

Mr. Snow returned to his desk, his knees bobbing. He removed a handkerchief from his shirt pocket and patted at the perspiration that had formed on his forehead.

Haley noticed the man's discomfort. "You worked with Mrs. Gray?" she asked.

Mr. Snow's gaze moved to the empty desk. "Yes. It's quite horrible, the whole incident."

"Did you like Mrs. Gray?" Samantha asked.

Mr. Snow sat back as if he'd been struck. "No, she was a married woman!"

Rather quick to assume I meant a romantic relationship, Haley thought.

Samantha's face showed her agreement with Haley.

"Did you like *working* with her," Samantha clarified.

"Oh, I'm sorry." Mr. Snow pulled on his collar. "She was a fine worker. Did her job the best she could, like the rest of us."

"Who else works in the office?" Haley asked.

"Mr. Tapper. He's on a coffee break. I can go get him if you like." Mr. Snow made to stand, and Haley waved for him to remain seated.

"Were you and Mrs. Gray involved?" Samantha

asked. "It's all right to speak frankly. Mr. Gray is being held for the crime."

Mr. Snow dropped into his desk chair and whimpered. "You can't tell anyone, please. I wanted to stop, but—".

"She didn't?" Haley said, finishing for him.

"Please, I'm not a home-wrecker. Besides, she had a son, and her husband was a mean son of a gun."

"Were you afraid of him?" Samantha asked.

"I'd be stupid not to be."

"Was Mrs. Gray afraid of him?" Haley asked.

"Olivia was one tough cookie. Braver than me by a long shot, I'm ashamed to say."

Haley believed it. "Did Mr. Gray ever visit Mrs. Gray at work?"

Mr. Snow's already pale face lost even more color. "Sometimes."

"Was he here four days ago?"

"I don't know. With the fire alarm and everything . . . he might've been, and no one noticed."

The office door opened wider, and an older man sauntered in with a mug of coffee and a cigarette hanging from the side of his mouth. His suit jacket had lost its sheen, and the white shirt which had come untucked from a fuller waist looked worn.

"Oh, who's this?"

Mr. Snow looked relieved to be out of the spotlight

and made quick introductions. "This is Miss Hawke from the paper and Dr. Higgins from the morgue, here about Olivia. This is Mr. Tapper."

"How d'you do?" Mr. Tapper went straight to his desk. "Wallace let you up the tower, eh? Must be your feminine charms."

Samantha frowned.

"Mr. Tapper," Haley said, "did you get along with Mrs. Gray?"

Mr. Tapper tapped ashes into his overly full ashtray. "I get along with most people. Turn a blind eye when I have to." He slid a look in Mr. Snow's direction and chuckled. "Can't believe her husband did it." He picked up a copy of the morning's *Boston Daily Record.* "Read about it in the papers."

Haley noticed Samantha squirm at that.

Mr. Tapper continued, "Never liked the swine."

"I understand she was up for a promotion," Samantha said.

Mr. Tapper scratched his nose. "So?"

"Who gets the promotion now?" Haley said.

"I do. But don't be getting no big ideas. I didn't kill Olivia. Her husband did." He stabbed the paper on his desk with a stubby finger. "Her crazy husband did."

17

Haley and Samantha were all but ushered out of Mr. Snow and Mr. Tapper's office by Mr. Tapper's glare alone. They rode the elevator back to the main floor in silence, neither of them wishing to discuss her thoughts in front of the liftboy.

Once they reached the lobby, Haley and Samantha stopped to talk.

"I think we should go to the police," Haley said.

"I suppose you're right. Do you think we could speak to Officer Bell?" Samantha ducked her head. "I sort of owe him."

Haley didn't have a problem with that. They stopped in at the receptionist's desk, daring Mr. Wallace's beady-eyed disapproval. Haley straightened to her full height and stared down at him.

"Might we borrow your telephone, Mr. Wallace," she said firmly. "It's a local call."

With no good reason to deny the assistant chief medical examiner, Mr. Wallace begrudgingly obliged. His face tightened when he heard Haley ask the operator to connect her to the police.

THEY MET at a sandwich shop near the police station. Tom Bell was already there and had just taken a bite of a toasted Reuben sandwich as they walked in. He grabbed a napkin to wipe his face then jumped to his feet.

"Hello, Dr. Higgins," he said. Haley noted that he let his gaze linger on Samantha when he greeted her. "Miss Hawke."

"Good afternoon, Officer Bell."

They sat at the round table, evenly spaced.

"I hope you don't mind I ordered already. I'm starved."

"Not at all," Haley said. "We'll order too." She noted Samantha's slightly panicked look. "On the morgue," she added. "It's business."

Samantha's shoulders softened slightly. The prompt waiter arrived to take their orders. Haley chose egg salad, while Samantha chose tuna.

"The reason we wanted to meet with you, Officer

Bell," Haley said, "is because both Miss Hawke and I, on separate occasions, received an anonymous tip regarding the Gray case."

"Oh?" Tom Bell's head swiveled from Haley to Samantha to Haley again. He lowered his sandwich. "What tips would these be?"

"I got a call at the paper," Samantha said. "The tipster said, 'she didn't jump.'"

"Okay," Tom said. "Male or female?"

"Female."

"Did she say how she knew?"

"No. She just said, 'she didn't jump' then hung up."

"And when was this?"

"The day after Mrs. Gray died."

"And I got a call at my home just this morning," Haley said. "According to her, Jacob Gray isn't responsible for his wife's death."

"What did she say exactly?"

"She said 'you got the wrong guy.'"

Haley and Samantha's order arrived, and they paused from their conversation.

Officer Bell's coffee arrived, and he took a sip. "Interesting," he said. "That'd explain why Detective Cluney's in such a foul mood. He doesn't have enough evidence to keep Gray in much longer, and the fellow refuses to confess."

"Maybe because he's not guilty," Haley said.

"But if not him," Officer Bell said, "Who?"

Haley leaned in. "We just returned from a visit to the Custom House. Both of the men who shared an office with Mrs. Gray have a motive for murder. Mr. Snow admits to having a short, but illicit affair, and Mr. Tapper has conveniently accepted the promotion that was going to go to Mrs. Gray."

"It would make sense that the killer had easy access to the window." Samantha lowered her sandwich. "There are a lot of simpler ways to kill a spouse if that was your intent."

Both Haley and Tom Bell stilled.

"Hey!" Samantha protested. "That wasn't a confession!"

Haley laughed. "Just checking."

Tom narrowed his eyes in thought. "Who is Mr. Wentworth?"

Samantha shook her head subtly at Haley, then said, "An inside source."

Haley frowned at Samantha. "He may be important."

"Fine," Samantha said with a huff of resignation. This meeting was not going how she'd imagined. "Mr. Richard Wentworth works in management at the Custom House. He and I went out for lunch."

Officer Bell narrowed his eyes. He leaned toward

Samantha and whispered out of the corner of his mouth. "I thought you weren't dating."

"I'm not. It was strictly business. Not that it's any of *yours*."

"I was present in the restaurant," Haley added quickly. She caught Samantha's look of gratitude.

"So, what else do you know about Mr. Snow and Mr. Tapper?" Tom asked.

"Mr. Snow and Mrs. Gray had an affair," Haley said.

"Scorned lover throws the object of his desire out of the window?" Tom Bell said. "Classic, 'if I can't have her, no one can' motive."

"Mr. Snow claimed it was her idea."

"He would now, wouldn't he?"

Officer Bell paid the check. "I've got it this time, ladies. You were right to bring this to me, but now you can move on to other things. Let the police take care of it." He hesitated by Samantha's chair as if he wanted to say more, but then left without another word.

Haley had been lost in her work at the morgue for a couple of hours. When the telephone rang, she took a moment to realize she was alone. Had Dr. Guthrie and Mr. Martin left for the day already? She hurried to the apparatus and picked up the receiver.

"Cluney here."

"Hello, Detective." Haley braced herself for another chewing out. No doubt Officer Bell's new information had set off his superior.

"Dr. Higgins. Officer Bell told me about your meeting earlier today, and the information you got from your source."

"Yes?"

"I thought it might interest you that, based on your information and motives of other possible suspects, and the fact that I hadn't enough evidence or a confession from Jacob Gray, I had to let him go. About an hour ago."

"I see." Haley was thankful for the call but found the detective's willingness to readily share things clearly filed under 'police business' rather suspicious. "Is there anything else?"

"In fact, there is. Another body."

Strange that Detective Cluney would leave that information to the end.

"Where should I meet you?"

A short pause. "I'm at the Custom House. It appears that Mr. Snow has jumped to his death."

18

Other than the time of day, it was a moment of déjà vu for Haley as she nudged her way through the rubbernecks to a mangled body smashed on the sidewalk below the tower of the Custom House.

Detective Cluney was there, along with Officer Bell and several other police officials that Haley recognized, including Officer Jack Thompson.

Jack smiled when he saw her, and Haley almost thought his look was wistful. She couldn't help but wonder if things would've turned out differently had they met in less tumultuous times.

"Hi, Jack," she said when she caught his eye.

"Evening, Doc," he returned. Then grimly. "Nasty stuff here."

"Two in a row," Haley said.

"Coincidence?"

"I'm not a believer in coincidence."

Detective Cluney approached. "Mr. Snow was the alleged lover of Mrs. Gray, right? He killed her, then suffering remorse, did himself in."

Haley took in the damage before her. Mr. Snow, much like Olivia Gray, appeared to have suffered greater upper body injuries than a feet-first jump would support.

"At first blush, I'd say he didn't go out of that window of his own accord, but I'll know more after the postmortem." Assuming the mayor didn't put a stop to this one, she thought. Waiting, she studied Detective Cluney's round face, but he did not object.

Haley tugged on her skirt and squatted beside the body, which was in similar grotesque condition to how Olivia Gray's had been.

Detective Cluney removed a cigarette from his coat pocket and lit up. After letting out a long stream of smoke, he said, "Pedestrians started screaming at six p.m., just after quittin' time."

Haley glanced at her wristwatch. Barely over an hour ago.

Detective Cluney stared blankly into space. "I let Gray go at five."

"Any word on where he is now?" Haley asked.

He shook his head. "I got guys looking for him."

Haley caught Officer Bell's eye. She and Samantha

had influenced Detective Cluney's decision to let Jacob Gray go. Haley's stomach flipped at the thought. She stared at the grim, wide-eyed look of the corpse in front of her. Was she, in part, responsible for this man's death?

No, Officer Bell had said the detective was short in both evidence and a confession to keep Jacob Gray. But, had a man died because they couldn't find the proof in time? The thought stabbed her.

Haley gazed at the growing crowd held back by the police and found the contingent of journalists. Samantha was nowhere in sight. She would be mad when she heard about this on the radio tonight, especially since Johnny Milwaukee was there, front and center with a big smile on his face. He adjusted his straw fedora and called out to her. "Dr. Higgins! Who jumped?"

Haley quickly looked away. Mr. Milwaukee knew she couldn't answer his questions anyway. For some reason, he seemed to want to be sure she saw him there.

She moved beside Officer Bell and spoke softly. "I don't see Miss Hawke here." She knew he was her inside tipster.

"I thought she got her information from Mr. Wentworth now."

"Officer Bell!" Haley said, surprised at the man's

pettiness. He seemed to read her thoughts and apologized.

"I'm sorry. Please don't tell her I said that. I couldn't call because I was already on the beat."

Officer Thompson had taken a roll of film of the crime scene, removed it from his camera, and inserted a new roll.

Haley approached him. "Can I get a copy of those photographs sent to the morgue?"

"Certainly. How are you, anyway, Haley?"

"I'm fine. Tired. I hope I didn't inadvertently contribute to setting a murderer free."

"You think Jacob Gray did this?"

"Don't you?"

"He's the most likely suspect. Cluney's gone in to question the employees who were still on the premises during the time frame of the fall. I'm going in to take photographs."

"Do you mind if I join you?"

"Not at all."

In the lobby, Detective Cluney questioned a young mail girl who pushed an empty mail cart.

Why is she still in the building after closing? Haley wondered. The girl looked frightened, but by the way she held herself—her shoulders slumped, her focus erratic—Haley wasn't certain her fear was directed at law enforcement. If not the police, then who was she afraid of? The killer?

Haley followed Jack into the elevator, and they headed up. When they entered the office, she was surprised to find Tapper at his desk.

"Dr. Higgins," he acknowledged with a grunt. "The cops won't let me go home. Told me to stay at my desk, so here I am."

Haley glanced at the officer stationed at the door. "I imagine Detective Cluney will be up shortly to interview you."

"Not that he'll learn anything from me. I wasn't in the room when Snow lost his head and decided to jump. He was smitten with that damn woman, you know. No dame is worth a topple to the cement. Dumb bird."

Being indoors, Jack Thompson prepared a flash pan. Smoke filled the room as he took new photographs. Haley wondered if they'd find anything new compared to the set taken immediately after Olivia Gray's death.

"Where were you when Mr. Snow jumped?" Haley asked.

"Not to be insensitive, *ma'am*, but I was in the john. I drink a lot of coffee. What of it? Just means he waited until I left the room to off himself. Mighty considerate of him, if you ask me."

19

Normally an early riser, Haley slept until the bells of her alarm clock chimed. Blindly, she reached for the disturbance and smacked the ringer off. She washed her face and brushed her hair, not an easy feat with her curls, and tied it loosely at the base of her neck. Thoughts of all that lay ahead of her filled her mind as she dressed in a tan and green formfitting cotton suit that flared slightly at her calves. Haley felt she was a little on the bony side to really fill these new styles out the way more curvaceous women, such as Samantha, could. It was a good thing the dead didn't care about such frivolous things as the latest in summer fashions.

In the kitchen, Haley joined Molly who was whistling over a pan of frying eggs.

"I'm going to pass on breakfast, Molly," Haley said as she reached for the coffee pot.

"Are you feeling all right, Dr. Higgins?"

"I overslept."

"Must've needed it," Molly said with a note of reproof. "You work too much."

"What can I say, Molly. I love work and work loves me."

"And what am I supposed to do with your eggs?"

Mr. Midnight pressed up against Molly's leg and meowed. Haley chuckled.

"I think you have your answer."

Haley filled her mug with hot percolated coffee and then headed to her office adjacent to the kitchen. Molly had retrieved the folded *Boston Daily Record* from the hallway and placed it on Haley's desk. News of the latest death blasted across the front page.

SECOND DEATH AT CUSTOM HOUSE

> The body of Mr. Philip Snow, 34, was discovered early last evening on the west side of the Custom House. Evidence suggests that Snow's death resulted from a fall from the seventh floor of the tower. Coincidentally, the very same floor and office window attributed to the fall and consequent death of Mrs. Olivia Gray only five days earlier.

> Police have yet to comment if the deaths are connected or if foul play is suspected. At the time of this writing there is no word from the coroner's office. Mr. Snow was in charting imports.
>
> Byline: Johnny Milwaukee

Haley grimaced. Samantha was sure to be sore about that, especially since she'd written up the first account. Officer Bell would have to smooth out a lot of feathers if he hoped ever to have a chance with Samantha Hawke.

She finished reading the rest of the paper as she drank her coffee, her mind on the death of Philip Snow. A murderer remained on the loose. Someone who likely knew she was poking her nose into the case. She wanted *him*, and he probably knew it.

She fished out a small key from the mix of paper-clips, unlocked the bottom desk drawer, and stared at the gun inside it, a Harrington & Richardson model 22 nine-shot pistol with a six-inch barrel and walnut checkered grip. Technically, it belonged in the morgue. The previous medical examiner had given it to her because of a rash of break-ins. After the last case, she'd brought it home.

Haley didn't like guns. It was too easy to pull the trigger, too easy to kill. But the weapon was also a good visual deterrent if you found yourself in a situation where you needed defense. She lifted it out of the drawer and made room for it in her purse.

At the mortuary, Haley was surprised to find that Dr. Guthrie had begun Mr. Snow's postmortem.

"Good morning," she said.

Dr. Guthrie grunted. "Dr. Higgins, good of you to join me."

Haley dropped her things on her desk, washed her hands, and donned a white apron. "You're rather eager today."

"Yes, well, it's been a while since I've got my hands dirty."

It was true that Haley's new boss had been reluctant to do his job, and she couldn't help but wonder if his sudden zest for life had something to do with his new friendship with Molly. She held in a smirk.

"What do you have here?" she asked.

"Broken bones, smashed skull. A mash of organs. Much the same as what you saw with Olivia Gray."

"So nice of the mayor to give the go-ahead for Mr. Snow's postmortem."

"Well, Dr. Higgins, now he has reason to believe foul play is in order, rather than a lady's emotional whim to throw herself out of the window."

Haley wanted to quip—had it been a man, the

natural conclusion that the flight from the seventh floor wouldn't have been emotional stress—but she had come to the quick assumption that Olivia Gray had committed suicide. Still, she'd wanted to perform the autopsy to give Mrs. Gray the benefit of the doubt.

"And your conclusions, Doctor?" Haley asked.

"This poor bloke did not fall feet first." He left the table to wash his hands, then stripped off his lab coat.

"If you'll be all right here alone, I'll be leaving for an hour or so."

"Of course, I'll be all right."

Haley turned to hide her grin. Could it be that Molly was his destination? She added, "Take your time."

"Indeed, I will."

Haley swore she could hear him whistling down the hall.

Dr. Guthrie left her to stitch up the Y incision, which she did with excellence, a task she'd done so often she could do it while sleeping. Mr. Martin wasn't around to help her lift the body onto the gurney, but this was also something she'd done many times on her own. She put her leg muscles into it, slid the corpse over, and pushed the gurney to the freezer cabinets. After pushing the body into an empty cabinet, she wrote out an identification card in her distinctive script —Philip Snow.

She'd just wrapped things up when Samantha blew into the morgue without bothering to knock.

"*He* took over my story! *He* didn't bother to call me to let me know. I had to hear about the death on the radio this morning!"

"You expected Mr. Milwaukee to call you?"

"No, Johnny took my story. *Tom* didn't call!"

"I'm just about to make coffee," Haley said. "Or maybe tea would be better?" Samantha was riled up, and caffeine might not be in her best interest.

"I'm not thirsty. I'm angry." Samantha dropped into the extra chair by Haley's desk. Haley put the kettle on anyway.

"Life's just not fair," Samantha said. "I'm only one person. I can't be everywhere all the time."

"No one expects you to be."

"*I* expect me to be."

Haley eyed the kettle and willed it to boil faster. "You're too hard on yourself, Samantha. And think about it; what exactly have you lost?"

"My story, obviously."

The kettle whistled, and Haley poured the hot water over the loose tea leaves in the teapot. "That particular story isn't over."

"Oh?" Samantha sat up as Haley placed the tea tray on her desk. "I heard that Mr. Gray pushed Mr.

Snow out the window, a final act of revenge for his wife's infidelity."

"Did Mr. Milwaukee tell you that?"

"He implied it." Samantha poured then added sugar to her tea. "Why? Do you know something he doesn't?"

"We can't be certain Mr. Gray did it," Haley said. "For one thing, no one has ever seen him in the building. A lot of people work there including janitors on every floor. Surely, someone would've spotted him. He doesn't exactly blend in. And for another, I don't think he loved his wife."

"Doesn't mean his ego didn't take a hit."

"That's true."

"Johnny says they're going to arrest him again."

"I don't doubt that."

"And you think the police got it wrong."

"I think the police don't have all the pieces to the puzzle."

"I don't think they have either. And Johnny's up to something."

Haley raised a dark brow. "Oh?"

"Two days ago, he put on this show of placing a file on his desk just before leaving the room. He practically begged me to snoop."

"And did you?"

"Of course."

"Anything of interest?"

"Just a list of two German names."

"German names?" Haley pulled in her chin. Since the end of the war, lists like that didn't exactly pique the public's interest. "What do you think it means?"

"I don't know. I mean, Johnny's not a war buff, not like some fellas I know. And besides, he's not a hobbyist. Everything is about the job. It has to be a lead."

"Do you think it's connected to the Gray case?"

Samantha shrugged. "I don't see how."

"Do you remember the names?"

"Yes. There were only two. And one of them is the same as my neighbor's son who was lost in the war. A Frieder Ginsberg. The other was Gerhardt Sommerfeld."

"Jacob Gray isn't his real name," Haley mused. "His mother is Mrs. Grabodski."

"Do you think he might have another alias?" Samantha said. "Such as Gerhardt Sommerfeld?"

"It's a stretch," Haley said, but then admitted, "but anything is possible, I suppose. Though, I can't imagine a Pole having a reason to masquerade as a German."

"Unless he's Jewish," Samantha said, grimly."

Haley conceded. Anti-Semitism was alive and well on both sides of the Atlantic. "I'll check in with Detective Cluney again."

Samantha left in much better spirits than when she'd arrived.

Haley put in a call to the police station.

Without saying hello, Detective Cluney said, "You've heard?"

"Heard what? Let me guess. You've arrested Jacob Gray again?"

"That's not why you called?"

"Well, sort of. Is it possible that Jacob Gray has an alias?"

"What do you mean?"

"Is it possible he's of German descent?"

"Not to my knowledge. Whatcha getting at?"

"Nothing. It's just a rabbit trail. I'm sorry to have disturbed you."

20

Replaying the latest developments in her mind, Samantha almost missed seeing Richard Wentworth as he crossed the busy street. She was about to call after him to say hello, but a bus rumbled by, and any effort at being heard or seen was futile. The dust kicked up by the thundering beast subsided as a timely break in traffic appeared, allowing Samantha to cross. In the back of her mind, she knew she was wasting time, but even though her lunch with Rick had been, on her end, business, she'd enjoyed his company. Perhaps this serendipitous sighting could lead to another meal, one quite personal. Of course, she wouldn't let it go anywhere it shouldn't. Not until her married status was officially changed to widowed, and there was always Talia to consider. But a friendly dinner exchanging pleasant, interesting conversation wouldn't hurt anyone.

Rick turned into a narrow, cobblestoned street, and Samantha wasn't sure she wanted to risk ruining the heels of her shoes. She couldn't even afford to take these back to the shoemaker, much less buy new ones. She'd just have to hope she'd run into Rick another time, or even better, now that he knew where she worked, he'd seek her out.

She'd decided to admit defeat when Rick unexpectedly stopped. He wasn't too far away now, and she'd just have to stay on the toes of her shoes. His back was to her. She raised her hand and was about to call out when another man suddenly appeared from behind a large trash collector.

How odd.

Curious, Samantha inched closer. If she stayed near the building's brick exterior, the trash bin would keep her out of the men's line of sight until Rick and the man parted ways. She didn't want to be rude by interrupting.

Her puzzlement grew as she watched them. Surely, it was a genial conversation, but why the furtive demeanor? Rick and his confidant were huddled close, hands in pockets, hats tipped forward as though they were sharing secrets and not simply talking about the weather.

Samantha held in a gasp. Richard Wentworth was speaking German. She knew enough about the language through Bina and the other German Jews who'd immigrated to Boston. *Was he saying something about Mexico?*

It wasn't a crime to speak German in Boston. Even though unrest remained in Europe since the war, it had no significant bearing on life in Boston.

Except Wentworth isn't a German name. His mother's side, maybe?

Instinctively, Samantha ducked behind the trash bin as the duo abruptly parted. Samantha held her breath, in part from the stench and in part from the fear—she was the curious cat about to be caught.

Both men exited the alley. When Samantha pushed away from the trash bin, she touched a particularly sticky and smelly spot with her fingers.

Drat!

Back on the main street, she entered a café and went straight to the restroom to wash her hands. Peering at her image in the mirror, Samantha adjusted her hat and patted her blond hair into place. Her face was flushed, and there was no going out in public with lips as pale as hers. She dug in her purse for her lipstick, applied it with slow, steady strokes, and smacked her red lips at her image.

Samantha let out a breath and hurried back

outside. If she didn't get back to the pit soon, she'd have some explaining to do. Mr. August was already questioning the time she spent away from the office with nothing to show for it. If she didn't come up with something substantial soon, he'd take her off the beat for good, and she'd be stuck writing the ladies' pages for the rest of her life.

21

Haley had learned from observing Detective Cluney that when the investigation stalled, the best thing to do was to go back to the beginning. Soon, she found herself parked along the curb on India Street, staring at the tower and counting the floors to the seventh. There was no way to slice it. A fall from that height was a death sentence. Two people had died violently: either a murder then a suicide, two suicides following each other, or two murders. Haley leaned toward the latter.

On impulse, she entered the Custom House and found Mr. Wallace behind the front desk.

"Hello, Mr. Wallace," she said pleasantly. "Long day?"

He dismissively rolled his eyes. "No more than any other day, Dr. Higgins."

"Have things quieted down, at least?"

He snorted. "The cops think they live here now. My throat is tired from all the questions, but I suppose you got a few more, or why would you be here."

"I thought maybe after some time had passed, something new might've come to mind."

"Why do you care? It's not your job, is it?"

"I see myself as an advocate for the dead."

Mr. Wallace shot Haley a surprised look. "I suppose someone ought to."

The female mail clerk Haley had seen Detective Cluney talking to pushed a full cart of mail toward the elevators. Haley thanked Mr. Wallace for his time and hurried after her.

"Miss?"

The mail clerk slowed to a stop and stared at Haley with a look of confusion. Thick-lensed glasses hid a pretty face. The name tag pinned to her light cardigan said, Miss Everson.

"Me?"

"I'm Dr. Higgins," Haley said when she'd caught up to her. "I'm the assistant chief medical examiner, and I'm wondering if you'd give me a moment of your time?"

Miss Everson's shoulders fell as she nodded. She didn't appear to be the type who'd try to defy an authority figure.

"Miss Everson, with your job delivering mail throughout the building, I imagine you know everyone?"

"It's a big building, Dr. Higgins. I'm not the only one who runs mail."

"Of course. Do you happen to deliver to the seventh floor?"

Miss Everson lowered her gaze. She nervously pushed on her glasses and said in a timid voice, "Why do you ask?"

"Did you deliver mail to Mrs. Gray and Mr. Snow's office?"

"I deliver mail to everyone on the seventh floor."

Haley tilted her head and smiled warmly, hoping to put poor Miss Everson at ease. "I imagine you hear things, see things that may not be quite on the up and up? On occasion?"

"I keep my nose to myself," Miss Everson said indignantly.

"But you must hear things, even when you're not trying to."

A look of apprehension flashed behind Miss Everson's eyes, and Haley turned to see the tempestuous Mr. Tapper heading for the elevators.

"Dr. Higgins," he said with a sour expression. "Doing the police's work for them, eh?"

"Hello, Mr. Tapper," Haley said, not rising to the bait. "I hear you got the promotion, in the end."

"Now look here—"

The bell of the elevator rang, interrupting whatever rude and misogynistic thing he was tempted to say. Two men dressed in business suits got off and Mr. Tapper stepped in. A quick glance at Miss Everson confirmed that she had no intention of getting into the elevator car with the man. The doors closed on him and Miss Everson let out a short breath.

"You don't like Mr. Tapper, do you?" Haley said.

"Why should I? I deliver mail to his office every day and it's like I'm invisible. Not a thank you, or how are ya? And he's not just like that with me, Dr. Higgins. As you can see, he has no love for any working woman."

"Like Mrs. Gray?"

Miss Everson finally looked Haley in the eye. She was about to say something when her face suddenly paled to a ghostly white. Her eyes latched on to something over Haley's shoulder.

Haley turned. Not some*thing*. Some*one*.

Miss Everson swallowed hard, then said, "Good afternoon, Mr. Wentworth."

"Sheila." Richard Wentworth tipped his hat at the mail clerk and winked. Miss Everson's pale face surged crimson. Haley did a double take at the look they shared along with his use of Miss Everson's Christian name. Definitely beyond the professional.

Mr. Wentworth grinned as he headed to the elevators, then shuddered to a stop. Pivoting, his blue eyes settled on Haley.

"You look familiar."

Haley stared back placidly. "I don't think we've met."

He snapped his fingers. "I remember now. You dined at the same restaurant as me the other day. You were with an older man, thinning hair, common face."

How rude of him to slight her companion unnecessarily. She sniffed and raised her chin. "I did go out with a friend the other day, but I'm afraid that I didn't notice you."

Richard Wentworth stepped closer. He was tall but not so tall that he looked down on her. She stared at him straight in the eyes. Closing the distance between them, he stood uncomfortably close. Haley forced herself not to step back.

"I think you did. In fact, I'm quite sure you were listening in on my conversation with my date."

Miss Everson choked back a small cough at this admission, and Haley had the feeling that the young, naive mail clerk had been on at least one date with Mr. Wentworth.

"The restaurant was crowded. But I could see how it would appear that way to someone like you."

He tilted his head. "Like me?"

"Yes. Someone who thinks he's a notch above everyone else."

Miss Everson gasped. Mr. Wentworth's mouth broke into a slow grin. He stepped away and tipped his hat. "Until we meet again, Dr. Higgins."

Haley stared, mouth gaping. How did he know her name? Clearly, Mr. Wentworth knew who she was before he'd begun the whole charade. But, why? Because his ego demanded that he be found attractive and wanted by every female in the city? She had to warn Samantha away from him.

Every evening was the same. On tired legs, Samantha trudged up two floors as she tried to ignore the implosion of dinner smells, which tonight seemed especially nasty. Like fish gone bad. Not an unusual odor in these parts considering how close the tenement building was to the fishing ports and the warehouses that cleaned the catch. It still never failed to make her throat want to close.

At least Bina's pot of matzoh ball soup smelled fine, if unexciting.

Talia drew at the kitchen table, and Samantha

swooped her up into her arms. "Missed you, honeybun!"

"Missed you too, Mommy. Look at my picture." A stick figure of a blond mother and daughter pair, along with a gray-haired granny.

Samantha wagered a guess. "Our family?"

Talia nodded and held her latest masterpiece in the air. "It's for you."

"Oh, thank you! It's beautiful."

Bina had her back turned to them as she stirred the soup.

"Mrs. Ginsberg forgot her reading glasses," Bina said. "Would you mind running them upstairs? Otherwise, she'll come when she finally notices they're not in her pocket, and she's the type who doesn't know when to leave."

Though Bina and Mrs. Ginsberg were both widows, at least Bina couldn't claim to be lonely. It wouldn't hurt her mother-in-law to show a little compassion, but Samantha would have to represent that for them both.

Mrs. Ginsberg lived one floor up and at the back of the hall. The O'Connors were having another row along with the shrieking cry of one of their babies. Samantha sighed. She hoped her "letter to the editor" would bring the problem to the public mind and perhaps spur change. She just had to make sure Mr.

August would run it.

Pushing on her thighs, Samantha made it to the next floor. The level of fitness to do all these stairs every day was worthy of admiration, especially in a lady like Mrs. Ginsberg, well into her senior years.

Samantha knocked when she reached the door, and when Mrs. Ginsberg didn't answer, she knocked harder. *Had Mrs. Ginsberg gone out*?

Samantha was about to turn away when the door cracked open, and Mrs. Ginsberg's frail voice said, "I don't want any."

"It's me, Mrs. Ginsberg. Samantha H—" Samantha almost said Hawke, but the Jewish community didn't know her by that name. "Samantha Rosenbaum."

The latch rattled as Mrs. Ginsberg released the lock, and the door swung open. "Oh, Mrs. Rosenbaum. Shalom. The Lord is gracious and good."

Samantha grinned. "Shalom."

"Come in, come in," Mrs. Ginsberg insisted.

"I've only come to return these." Samantha held out the glasses.

"Oh, dear. I would miss those when it came time to read the Torah. Thank you."

"You're welcome." Samantha turned, but Mrs. Ginsberg spoke before she could leave.

"Would you like to come in for tea?"

Samantha offered a polite smile. "I'm afraid I can't. My mother-in-law has dinner ready."

Mrs. Ginsberg's watery eyes flashed with disappointment. Her loneliness was almost tangible.

"But maybe I could have something cold to drink?" Tea preparation would take longer than Samantha could spare, but a few extra minutes to visit with the older woman wouldn't hurt. Besides, Bina was used to Samantha being late for dinner.

Mrs. Ginsberg's eyes brightened. "Water? Or, I might have a bottle of Coca-Cola in my icebox."

"Water is fine."

Mrs. Ginsberg disappeared into her kitchen leaving Samantha in the small living room furnished with old pieces that a person could either consider antique or just plain worn-out. Much like her own apartment, there wasn't a spot of dust to be found. Even the windows had been scrubbed clean.

A black-and-white photo of a young man sat on a faded buffet cabinet. Samantha picked up the frame and studied it with a frown.

She jumped when Mrs. Ginsberg spoke. "That's my son, Frieder. Wasn't he such a handsome young man?"

"When was the last time you saw your son, Mrs. Ginsberg?"

Mrs. Ginsberg's expression fell. "Back before the

war. We lived in Berlin when the war broke out. Mr. Ginsberg was already gone, and my sister Ruth lived in Boston. She begged me and Frieder to come before Frieder was forced to fight. Frieder refused to leave his country, but he insisted that I come to America. He promised me he'd join me after the war." Her lined lips quivered. "He never did." She glanced up with watery eyes. "He died a hero."

Samantha nodded in sympathy for the woman's loss, though she didn't think her son had died a hero. All she knew was the man in the photograph was a younger version of the man she'd seen with Richard Wentworth in the alley earlier that day, and was very much alive.

HALEY COULDN'T HELP but feel unnerved by her encounter with Richard Wentworth. She'd met a lot of self-important men in her lifetime, but Mr. Wentworth was the king among a muster of peacocks. She hated how he'd rattled her, but silently patted herself on the back for not backing down.

Sheila feared the man. Why? Was he simply a bully who liked to play with women's hearts?

Or was it more?

While Haley had been indoors, clouds had rolled in creating an earlier sense of twilight than the norm.

The adrenaline rush of standing up to Mr. Wentworth subsided, and a wave of fatigue took its place. It was still light enough to take the shortcut through the alley to her car.

The lane opened up to an empty lot. The wind stirred, and Haley could smell the promise of a thunderstorm in the air. Holding on to her hat, she headed through the tufts of wild grass. She caught a glimpse of something along the broken-down fence line.

A shadow. The shape of a man? Mr. Wentworth?

Haley's heart thudded large in her chest. How stupid of her to take the lane alone at this time of night.

She could keep walking, *should* keep walking, but if Mr. Wentworth thought he could frighten her away, he was wrong.

Haley slipped her hand into her purse, her fingers clasping the handle of her gun.

She called out, "Who's there?"

The shadow stilled but remained silent.

Haley removed the gun from the bag and pointed. "I tell you, I'll shoot."

"Okay, okay," the form said. He raised his hands and stepped out of the shadows. "I'm unarmed and didn't mean to frighten you."

Haley let her arm go slack. "Mr. Milwaukee?"

22

Samantha shared a bed with her daughter and had just finished with the bedtime story. Prayers, a glass of water, questions about why the sky was blue and where elephants came from were completed. Talia released an angelic-type yawn, before finally closing her eyes and drifting to sleep.

Rain splattered against the windows in a sleep-inducing rhythm. Samantha allowed her eyelids to close, though she knew she had only a few minutes. She couldn't very well fall asleep in her clothes, and besides, it was too early to go to bed. She'd be awake before dawn if she succumbed to her sleepiness now.

As she slipped from Talia's tender hold, she heard the sharp rap of knuckles on the door, followed by Bina's aging voice.

"Who is it?"

Samantha was in the hallway, closing her bedroom door, when the answer resounded thickly from the other side. "Messenger boy!"

"I'll get it," Samantha said, waving Bina to step aside. There were several locks on the door, and Samantha opened the two bolts but left the chain hooked. A quick peek into the vestibule proved the veracity of the announcement. A boy of about thirteen with wet cheeks and a dripping-wet flat cap stood waiting. Samantha released the chain.

"Yes?"

"A message from a lady doctor, ma'am."

"Oh!" Filled with curiosity. Samantha took the envelope from the boy, fished out a penny from her skirt pocket, and offered it as a tip. He ran off, and she closed the door behind him.

Bina shuffled close. "What is it?"

"It's a note from Dr. Higgins." Samantha peeled the envelope open. First, she wondered how Haley had known where she lived. Then she hoped everything was all right.

"What's it say?" Bina asked. "What does she want?"

Samantha frowned. "She's requesting that I join her and a colleague from work for a coffee."

Bina snorted. "It's too late for coffee. You'll never sleep. Besides, it's dark, and the weather is atrocious.

What kind of friend sends an invitation like that—so last minute and at night? That takes a lot of *chutzpah*!"

Bina opened the hall door and shouted. "You, boy! Come back!"

Samantha tugged her mother-in-law by the arm and pulled her back inside.

"Don't do that."

"Why? What? Don't tell me you plan on going?"

"Dr. Higgins wouldn't call for me if it wasn't important."

"Important, how? Important enough to risk your life? Does she know you can't afford to take a taxi whenever and wherever you like? At least she could've had the decency to come to you in person."

Samantha didn't want any of her friends to come in person. The tenements weren't something she wanted to show off.

Though Haley knew where she lived, well, at least Johnny didn't need to know. That was why Haley hadn't come in person, Samantha deduced. She was with Johnny and wanted to preserve Samantha's dignity. Samantha was thankful for that.

"I can afford a taxi once in a while," Samantha said, as she gathered her coat, hat, and gloves. "Besides, this is work related. My boss will compensate me."

"*Meshugge!* You are crazy!"

Samantha retrieved her umbrella from the coat rack. "I'll be fine, Bina. You worry too much."

"And you don't worry enough."

The coffee shop wasn't that far away, and if it hadn't been for the pouring rain, Samantha could've walked. As it was, she wondered if they'd get there in one piece. Even with the *swatch, swatch* of the windshield wipers, she could hardly make out the road in front of her. How the taxi driver did was a miracle.

She paid the driver, wished him a safe night, and opened her umbrella. It was only a few steps to the front door, but the effort saved her hat.

Inside, she released the hold on her umbrella and dropped it into the umbrella stand by the door. Her eyes scanned the long and narrow room and landed on Haley and Johnny sitting in a booth at the back. It was odd seeing both of them chatting together as if two of her worlds had meshed together in some unnatural way.

"Hello," she said when she reached them. She took the empty spot beside Haley. "What's up?"

Johnny snorted. "Your friend here almost killed me."

Samantha shot Haley a look. "What?"

"I didn't even fire my gun," Haley said dispassionately. "You shouldn't be following ladies through empty lots in the dark."

Samantha put a palm up. "Wait. What am I missing?"

"Mr. Milwaukee was following me."

Samantha almost jumped out of her bench seat. "You dirty shyster! You're trying to steal my story!"

"Hold your horses, doll." Johnny's lips pulled into that aggravating, alluring side grin. *Drat the man*! "We're on the same team."

"Like heck we are!"

A youthful waitress suddenly appeared, and Samantha checked her emotions. She must remain professional.

"Can I get you something?" the girl asked.

"No, I'm fine."

"Go on," Johnny said. "It's on my bill."

"Then definitely not."

"Bring her a tea," Haley said, then to Samantha, added, "It'll calm your nerves."

Samantha ruffled at the presumption that her nerves needed calming, but she protested no further.

"Mr. Milwaukee has been pursuing a different story, Samantha," Haley said, "and it seems our leads and his are intersecting."

Samantha pursed her lips. "Oh?"

Johnny lit a cigarette and released a stream of

smoke out of the side of his mouth in the opposite direction.

"It's about your boyfriend, Richard Wentworth."

Samantha scowled and was about to tell Johnny off when her tea arrived. "Milk and sugar, ma'am?"

"Yes, please."

Haley had been correct. The tea did calm her, and gave her something to do with her hands when the urge to pound the table or punch Johnny in the nose became too strong.

Once the waitress had departed, Johnny said, "Mr. Wentworth is an interestin' individual."

"I could've told you that," Samantha replied sharply.

"He's a spy."

Samantha choked on her tea. After patting her lips with a napkin, she looked to Haley.

"What's he talking about?"

"His name's on the list."

"What list? Oh, the German names?"

Haley nodded. "According to Mr. Milwaukee, Wentworth is an alias for Gerhardt Sommerfeld."

Samantha felt like she'd been slapped. Why did she always fall for the wrong type of man!

"Are you sure, Johnny? How do you know?"

23

Haley felt bad for Samantha who had circles under her eyes from lack of rest. The burden of responsibility carried radiated across to Haley in waves. It made her own life seem simple: she had no dependents, and only Molly's wages to pay out of her own. Good fortune in an inheritance, combined with good intuition to get out of the markets before they crashed, had allowed her to pay cash for her nice apartment. Haley had only sent the messenger boy because she wanted to help Samantha out. She knew how competitive the newspaper business was, and in particular, how competitive Samantha was with Johnny Milwaukee. Samantha would never have forgiven Haley if she hadn't included her.

"Mr. Milwaukee?" Haley said, encouraging him to

answer Samantha's question. "Tell her what you told me."

Johnny stubbed out his cigarette, furtively checked over each shoulder, leaned in and lowered his voice. "Let me back up. Sommerfeld—or Wentworth, as we know him—arrived in New York near the beginning of the war in fourteen on the merchant cargo ship SS *Iserlohn*."

Samantha lightly slapped the tabletop. "I knew it. That's why you suddenly liked my pen. I did a little digging on that myself, Johnny." Her smile was smug. "Woodrow Wilson didn't let those ships leave port under the guise of doing them a favor, but today, mass opinion is that he was already in cahoots with the British."

Johnny stared back with a look of surprise and a note of admiration.

"Very good, Sam. Once the German government realized that Woodrow Wilson was holding their sailors captive, our boy Sommerfeld was instructed to use them to stir up mischief."

"Why was that?" Samantha asked.

Johnny tapped ash into the ashtray. "Retaliation. You see, Wilson's order left thousands of German sailors stranded on their ships. Most were still very tied to the homeland and were interested in Germany's victory."

"So, you're saying that Wentworth organized mischief groups?"

Johnny nodded. "Some call them terrorist cells. It wasn't hard amongst all those bored sailors eager for a fight."

"What did he possibly hope to accomplish?"

"Well," Haley started, "the logic of the German government—and this was a very narrow logic—was if the Americans were worried about what was happening here at our own munitions factories, subways, and bridges . . . if America feared what happened along the home front, then we wouldn't have the time or the will to fight in a war across an ocean. We'd be too busy with our own problems."

Johnny grunted. "As if we'd be dumb enough to fall for that."

"What kind of *mischief* did they get into?" Samantha asked.

"Sommerfeld organized small cigar bombs on ships," Johnny said, "which killed hundreds of American sailors and civilians. They also blew up the Dupont Plant in New Jersey."

Samantha shifted uncomfortably. "Is that why you wrote an anniversary story on it?"

"It's the story that got me digging, doll. Soon, I discovered that Sommerfeld was the ringmaster of a large terrorist ring. When the United States entered the war in 1917, and in particular when the SS *Housatonic*, a large cargo liner, was sunk by a German U-boat, Sommerfeld knew that it would get too dangerous to remain active in the US. He fled to Mexico."

"He and Frieder Ginsberg were talking about Mexico," Samantha said. "They were talking about Mexico just this morning."

Johnny leaned in. "Wait a minute. How do you know about Ginsberg? He's a ghost."

"I happened to overhear them speaking in German."

Johnny leaned back, his narrowed-eyed gaze latching on to Samantha. "You just happened to overhear?"

"How I heard is not important!"

"Do you remember what he said?" Haley asked.

"No. I don't know German. I just made out the word *Mexico*. It didn't seem significant at the time," Samantha said.

Johnny pressed, "How do you know the man he met is Ginsberg?"

"As it so happens, his mother lives in my building. I returned an item to her this evening and saw his picture in her apartment. She thinks her son is dead."

"I don't understand the interest in Mexico," Haley said. "They were neutral during the war."

"Many Germans guilty of war crimes fled to Mexico after they lost the war," Johnny said. He tapped his shirt pocket. "That's what the list is about. Now that this Hitler guy has formed a popular nationalist party, it appears guys like this are resurfacing."

THOUGH DR. GUTHRIE sat at his desk on the other side of the glass wall—drinking tea, compliments of Mr. Martin—she could hear him *whistling*. Haley didn't know if she preferred this joyous version of Dr. Guthrie over the cantankerous one. It was hard enough to focus on her paperwork. She couldn't shake what she had learned about the war last night. She'd spent two years in France, patching up the wounded from both sides. Many German soldiers, so young they barely shaved, had simply been following orders.

A decade later, Germany was still in rubble and economic straits. At the time, Haley had felt that the judgments laid against the nation were just, but perhaps too harsh. The last thing the world needed was another Kaiser-type leader to stir up war. Haley kept abreast of the news coming out of Europe. She had a feeling this Hitler fellow would cause trouble.

"What do you think, Dr. Higgins?"

Haley turned to the voice of her young intern. "What is it, Mr. Martin?"

Thomas Martin stepped aside to reveal the repaired skeleton. "Ta-da."

Haley gave the teaching skeleton a good examination. Mr. Martin had done a fine job of patching the breaks and smoothing the scars down. Close inspection didn't conceal the trauma the skeleton had endured at her hands, but when she stepped back a few feet, she could say it wasn't worse for wear.

"Good job, Mr. Martin."

"Thank you, Dr. Higgins. I wouldn't recommend subjecting it to any more abuse though. I don't think it could be repaired a second time."

"Let's hope we never have reason to do so."

Considering the skeleton's plight brought Haley's thoughts back to the death of Olivia Gray. A wave of guilt washed over her. Mr. Milwaukee's new lead about German spies had overshadowed her case. She corrected herself—her efforts to assist Detective Cluney to solve his case. Haley hated the thought that anyone whose life was suddenly ended and violently so, would be buried without justice being served. Someone had pushed Olivia Gray out of the window, and Mr. Snow, as well.

As a courtesy, Haley knocked on Dr. Guthrie's door before stepping into the room.

"Do you need me for anything, Dr. Guthrie?"

He grunted, and Haley smiled. The "old" Dr. Guthrie had returned.

"Why?" he asked. "Are you taking time off again?"

Haley was paid a salary—so as long as her duties in the morgue were properly performed, her time was her own.

"Just for a short while. Hopefully, no one will die while I'm gone." *Heaven forbid that Dr. Guthrie attended a crime scene for once.*

"I suppose Mr. Martin can handle things here."

"Very well."

Something told Haley she needed to keep digging on Jacob Gray, and more precisely, the marriage of Jacob and Olivia Gray. There was more to his story, she was sure of it, and her quest led her to City Hall.

She found a parking spot on School Street and gazed up at the impressive-looking Baroque-style building. At the top of a set of cement steps, a heavy wooden door with a rounded frame was flanked by a set of Romanesque pillars.

The humidity followed Haley inside, and although shaded from the sun, there was little respite offered. The fans hung from high ceilings and whirled frantically with minimal effect.

The gentleman on the other side of the information desk smiled at her. "Hello, ma'am. How may I help you?"

Taking a cue from the man's name tag, Haley said, "Mr. Peele, I'm Dr. Haley Higgins, the city's assistant chief medical examiner." Haley found if she established her authority up front, it was much more likely that she'd get the cooperation she sought.

"I'm happy to assist, Dr. Higgins."

"I'd like access to a marriage document."

Mr. Peele led Haley into a room furnished with several tables. A clerk manned the file cabinets that filled a connecting room.

"This is Miss Olsen," Mr. Peele said. "She'll help you search for what you're looking for."

Miss Olsen, a petite woman with bright, intelligent eyes, had chestnut hair with several strands of gray. The wrinkles around her mouth and eyes pointed to an age somewhere in the mid-forties.

Haley repeated her introduction. "I'd like to see the marriage license for Jacob and Olivia Gray."

"Very well," Miss Olsen said. "What year?"

"1925, I believe."

"Please, wait here," Miss Olsen said, then disappeared into the file room.

As she waited, Haley mentally reviewed what she knew about Olivia Gray. Employed by the Custom House before she married Jacob, she had a five-year-old son born in '26, a year after they wed. Or, at least one calendar year. Had she, as Samantha had suggested, already been with child on her wedding day? Was that why she'd married Jacob Gray? Was she so unhappy in the marriage that she'd turned to Mr. Snow for comfort? Had Jacob Gray killed her, and subsequently Mr. Snow, for it?

Miss Olsen returned with a look of confusion on her face.

"Are you sure the name is Gray? I found nothing in our files for a Jacob and Olivia Gray in 1925. I also checked the preceding and following years, and there's nothing."

"Try the name Grabodski," Haley said.

Miss Olsen returned a short time later with a smile on her face and a file in her hand. "I believe I found it." She handed it to Haley.

"You may return it to me before you leave."

"I will, Miss Olsen. Thank you."

The file contained a single marriage license. Haley frowned as she read the names. Jacob Grabodski and Olivia Sommerfeld.

Sommerfeld? What an odd coincidence.

"Miss Olsen?"

The clerk's head bobbed up as Haley carried the file over.

"Yes?"

"Would you mind looking for another file for me?"

"If I can?"

"Do you have any information on Olivia Sommerfeld? Perhaps immigration documents?"

"We cross-reference everything, Dr. Higgins. It may take a while, but I'll see what I can find."

Miss Olsen proved excellent at her job and returned with a file sooner than either of them thought possible.

"This is immigration documentation for a Mrs. Olivia Sommerfeld," she said.

Haley returned to the table and opened the file.

How interesting!

Mrs. Olivia Sommerfeld immigrated from England in 1922. Alone. Her status listed as "*widow*."

A handwritten notation at the bottom of the file stated that Mrs. Sommerfeld (née Hayes) had once lived in Germany where she had married a man called Gerhardt Sommerfeld.

Olivia Gray and Richard Wentworth were once married.

24

Johnny had made Samantha promise not to tell anyone about his quest to unveil possible traitors to America, but she'd spent a sleepless night considering how dangerous this information was. There were moments while listening to Talia's soft breathing that she resented Johnny for this revelation. Why had he saddled her with it?

Or maybe the fault should lie with Haley? She was the one who had invited her into the circle. Knowing Haley wanted to use the information to frighten Samantha into staying away from Wentworth, rather Gerhardt Sommerfeld, Samantha realized it had worked.

It was hard to concentrate on pages the next day, and when Johnny failed to show up at the pit, she found her stomach flipping with concern. If Johnny knew about them, there was a good chance they knew about him.

"Hey, Max," she called out when the timid man entered the room. Samantha never did understand how a man of his temperament worked in the newspaper business. There was a reason they called it the pit. It was a constant dog fight to get to the top, even if the barking could only be heard from a distance.

"Miss Hawke?"

"Have you seen Johnny lately?"

"Not since yesterday."

Samantha caught the eye of the other fellows in the room, but she was only met with shaking heads. The boisterous Freddy Hall didn't even stop pecking at his typewriter.

She was almost ready to report to Mr. August and suggest he call the police when Johnny strolled in.

"Where were you?" she demanded.

"Well, Ma, I met a girl, and we got busy. Sorry I missed curfew."

Samantha crumpled a piece of paper into a ball and threw it at him. "You cad!"

Johnny grinned his stupid crooked smirk and leaned over her desk. "Were you worried about me, doll?"

"Go away."

"You were, weren't you? I knew you were secretly in love with me."

"In your dreams. Now leave. Can't you see I'm busy?"

Johnny peered at the paper in Samantha's typewriter before she could do anything to hide it.

"Spaghetti with Boiled Carrots and White Sauce."

"Leave her alone, Johnny."

Both Johnny and Samantha stilled at Max's voice.

"Ah, I think we have a love triangle, doll."

Samantha narrowed her eyes. "Shut up and go away."

"Very well."

Samantha half expected him to toss her a one-line teaser, just to drive her crazy, but maybe Johnny hadn't discovered anything new since their visit with Mrs. Ginsberg the night before.

Good.

Her fingers hovered, and she let out a breath of frustration. Johnny worked on breaking a story about Great War terrorists while she reported how to make the most out of potatoes and hot dogs. She finished the piece on "Feeding your Family on a Dime," and handed it to Mr. August. The thought of spending another minute at her desk, especially with Johnny typing away at who-knew-what, made her fidgety. Since breaking a big story, Mr. August had given her free rein over her time. She'd walk around town and see if a story would find her.

She strolled down State Street toward the docks and had only been strolling five minutes when a familiar figure headed her way. Her heart jumped. Belatedly, she searched for a way to conceal herself, but Richard Wentworth, alias Gerhardt Sommerfeld, had clearly spotted her.

"Miss Hawke," he called.

Samantha froze as a chill raced down her spine. Her heart thudded loudly in her chest and she swallowed dryly. A war criminal was heading towards her.

Stay calm. She was an investigative reporter, for crying out loud! Pretend to be undercover. Maybe, if she was smart and a little lucky, she'd get information she could use to bargain with Johnny.

She forced a smile. "Mr. Wentworth."

He smiled in return. "You're a hard lady to find."

"Oh. You've been looking for me?"

"Well, I'd hoped we'd run into each other. I wondered if you'd be interested in going out for dinner again."

Samantha kept the smile in place. "That would be lovely, but I'm quite booked this week."

"Next week, then?"

"Sure."

"Great. Are you walking somewhere? Maybe I could join you."

"Just getting air." Samantha decided the truth wouldn't hurt. "I'm hoping to come across a news story. Being in the right place at the right time can make my job easier."

"Boston is a colorful place. I'm sure you can find an interesting story if no one decides to rob a bank today."

What a charming smile. Too bad he was such a devil! "I'm sure you're right."

"By the way, how is that jumper story going?"

Samantha eyed him slyly. "The coroner's office is quite certain the victim was murdered. She and her colleague. Surely, you've read the papers."

"Of course. I just thought maybe you had heard something new. People at the office are rather upset, as you can imagine. I'd hoped you'd have something encouraging for me to share. Do you know if they've got a suspect in sight?"

Before Samantha could come up with an answer, Haley drove by in her DeSoto and waved at them through the window.

"Miss Hawke!"

Haley pulled to the curb, stepped out, and approached them.

Samantha gave her a questioning look.

Irritation at being interrupted flashed briefly behind Wentworth's eyes. "Good day, Dr. Higgins."

"I hope you don't mind if I steal Miss Hawke away? Her boss contacted the morgue looking for her."

"We're friends, you see," Samantha explained. "We often have lunch."

"Quite," Richard said. "She looks very much like a patron who sat near us on our first date."

Samantha froze at her misstep. She *really* had to learn how to keep her stories straight!

"I understand the demands of work," Wentworth said, obviously choosing to ignore her faux pas. "I must return to my office as well." He tipped his hat. "Until next week, Miss Hawke."

Once he was out of sight, Haley spoke tersely in Samantha's ear. "There is no way on God's green earth that you're going on another date with that man."

25

"I have no intention of going on another date with that dirty shyster."

Haley let out a breath of relief. One thing she'd learned about Samantha Rosenbaum in their short friendship was that she could be obstinate, nearly matching Haley's capacity for stubbornness.

"I'm glad to hear it," Haley said as she led Samantha westward by the elbow. "Because I've just learned that Mr. Wentworth, also known to us as Herr Sommerfeld, was once married to Olivia Gray."

Samantha stopped short and stared at Haley in disbelief. "You can't be serious!"

"It's true." As they walked, Haley relayed her recent visit to the city hall and what she'd discovered there."

Samantha pinched her lips together. "That swine."

"It's means motive, and opportunity," Haley said. "He has the physical strength to overpower his wife—we can presume she discovered something unsavory that he didn't want getting out, and he works at the Custom House."

"I should know this, but how long has the swine worked at the Custom House anyway?" Samantha asked.

"Not long. Only three weeks."

"What was it, I wonder," Samantha said, "that Olivia discovered? Other than the man she'd hoped to escape had found her once again."

"Or perhaps, she found him," Haley mused. "She was listed as a widow on her immigration papers. She may have been led to believe her husband had died."

"Can you imagine her shock to arrive at work one day and find her 'dead husband' standing there?"

"I'll bet it was a shock for both of them. And if Herr Sommerfeld wanted to keep his alias hidden..."

Samantha finished for her. ". . . He'd want to silence his wife for good."

"We mustn't jump to conclusions, though," Haley said. "With the arrival of Mr. Wentworth, Mrs. Gray's marriage to Jacob Gray would be null and void."

"Which would mean their son would be illegitimate."

"Which would give Jacob motive, once again. Take out his wife before the fallacy was discovered."

Samantha realized that Haley was leading their steps. "Where are we going?"

"To the police station," Haley said. "It's time to share notes with Detective Cluney."

OFFICER BELL GREETED them when they arrived, and Haley could feel the tension radiate between Samantha and the policeman. Poor fellow. There was nothing worse than unrequited love.

"Is Detective Cluney in?" Haley asked. "It's regarding the Gray and Snow cases."

"If you'll wait here for a moment, I'll let him know you're here."

Haley and Samantha sat on the wooden chairs near the opened door, and Samantha removed her hat to fan herself with it. Haley had an intuition that the sudden flush of heat her friend suffered from wasn't only from the temperature outdoors.

Haley lowered her voice to not attract the attention of the other civilians in the waiting area. "You should put the man out of his misery."

"What do you mean?"

"He's clearly smitten. Either let him take you out on a date or get a new informant."

Samantha scoffed. "Like it's so simple to get an informant."

"Then go on a date."

"And lead him on?"

Haley raised a dark brow. "Are you not attracted to him at all?"

"He's handsome, kind, and has a respectable job."

"But he's not Johnny Milwaukee."

"Dr. Higgins!"

Haley bit back a grin. "I've obviously hit a nerve."

"I am *not* interested in Johnny. He's a colleague and an annoying one at that. You know my situation. Not only am I still legally married, but I also have Talia to think about."

"Of course, I'm sorry," Haley said. She felt a stab of remorse at taking her jesting too far.

"But maybe, after . . ." Samantha stared ahead blankly, not finishing her thought.

"After?" Haley prompted, her curiosity getting the best of her again.

"Once Seth has been declared dead. Talia deserves a father. Tom Bell would do well."

Haley was about to chime in on her thoughts of getting married to someone she didn't love to provide a father figure for her daughter when they were interrupted by the man himself.

"He'll see you now, ladies," Tom said.

Samantha returned her hat to her head, then smiled. "Thank you, Tom."

Haley noted Samantha's use of Officer Bell's first name, and couldn't stop the sense of concern that washed over her.

Inside Detective Cluney's office, Haley and Samantha each took one of the wooden chairs facing the detective's desk. Haley wasted no time with pleasantries and got right to relaying everything she and Samantha had learned.

Detective Cluney leaned back in his leather chair and tented his fingers.

"So, let me get this straight. You're trying to tell me that a manager at the Custom House, Mr. Richard Wentworth, a guy with official papers confirming that he's a former British citizen and now an American citizen, is a German spy?"

Haley pushed down the anger she felt at the sound of condescension in the detective's voice.

"Spies from any country are masters at covering their footsteps and masquerading as aliases."

"And you got your information from—no, don't tell me—a confidential informant."

Samantha jutted out her chin. "We gained the information from a well-respected colleague of mine who's been following the story."

"Ah, a reporter, eh?" Cluney retrieved a cigar

from the ornate wooden cigar box on his desk. "No offense, ma'am, but reporters aren't exactly trustworthy."

"We're merely trying to do our jobs, Detective, the best we can," Samantha said. "Much like you and your officers, I gather."

Haley wanted to shake Samantha's hand to congratulate her pluck.

"Miss Hawke," Detective Cluney said, growing red at the neck from Samantha's chastisement. "Like I said. No offense."

Haley stepped in before Samantha could say something she'd regret. "Detective Cluney, even if the chance of this information is slight, isn't it worth pursuing? I'm under the assumption that your leads have dried up. Olivia Gray had once been married to a Gerhardt Sommerfeld, and if Richard Wentworth and Mr. Sommerfeld are the same, that is motive."

Detective Cluney snipped the end of the cigar and lit it. "Why would he kill his ex-wife?"

"There are several possible reasons," Samantha said. "Olivia Gray may not have known her former husband was still alive, and he wanted to keep word of that from getting out."

"Or," Haley added, "she might've decided to blackmail him."

"Very well." Detective Cluney filled the room with

aromatic smoke. "I'll give you a man." He directed his shout out the opened door. "Bell!"

Apparently, Officer Bell was hovering nearby because he was inside the detective's office in an instant. "Yes, sir."

"Listen to what Dr. Higgins and Miss Hawke have to say about the Gray case and give them whatever assistance you can."

"Yes, sir."

The detective waved thick fingers in dismissal, but then added, "I'll need a confession."

"That guy's ruthless," Samantha said as they left the building. She cast a glance at Tom Bell who dutifully followed.

"He's a busy man," Tom said. "I hope you're not wasting his time."

"Do you doubt our report?"

"I'm more doubtful of your source."

"You were eavesdropping!"

If Tom was trying to get on my good side, Samantha thought, *he was doing a poor job of it.*

"When the boss leaves the door open, it means he wants someone to pay attention."

Samantha didn't miss Haley rolling her eyes as she broke through the bickering.

"Let's get a coffee, shall we, and discuss this like professionals."

Haley was always the reasonable one whereas Samantha knew she let her emotions get the best of her at times. Like now, when she inexplicably felt both annoyed and buoyed by Tom's presence.

The coffee shop, a narrow, little hole in the wall with a row of booths along one side and a row of round matching stools along a counter on the opposite wall, was filled with the strong yet comforting smell of coffee and cigarettes. Samantha had fond childhood memories of being treated to salted taffy from the glass bowl by the register when she came in with her grandfather.

They selected the last booth at the end for optimum privacy, ordered coffee, and waited for the waitress to pour and deliver their orders. Tom heaped two teaspoons of sugar into his coffee and stirred.

"Okay," he said once the waitress had left. "Let's say I believe Milwaukee, that he's not just stringing you gals along for his amusement, and Wentworth is also Sommerfeld. What do we do about it? You heard the boss. He wants a confession."

"Then we have to get one," Samantha said. The indignation she felt over Wentworth pulling the wool over her eyes fueled her determination. "He wants to take me out on another date. I should let him."

In unison, Haley and Tom shouted, "No!"

Samantha pulled back as if she'd just been blown against the brick wall by a gale force wind. The surrounding patrons stretched their necks in their direction.

"Hear me out," she finally said. "We won't do anything dangerous. Besides, we'll be in a public place."

"Even if you did manage to get him to confess," Tom said, "it'd just be your word against his. We'd have to record it somehow, and we can't set that up in a public place."

"What if we used my place," Haley said. Samantha smiled. Good, they were on the same team.

"Wentworth doesn't know where I live—"

Tom cut in. "You don't know that. If he's an international war spy, he's bound to have done his homework on you."

"He's right," Haley said. "However, you could say that you're staying at a friend's house while she's away. That you're taking care of my plants and cat."

"Wait a minute," Tom said. "We have to assume this guy has ulterior motives." To Samantha, he quickly added, "Not that you aren't desirable, but if he's checked up on you, he'll know you're married and have a daughter."

Samantha gulped. The thought of a man like Wentworth-Sommerfeld knowing about Talia so that he might insert himself into her life, frightened her. Enough to make sure nothing like that could ever happen.

"He wants to know what I know about Olivia Gray. Or more accurately what I think the police know."

Tom let out a breath. "That makes sense. A man like that thrives on information. What if Samantha got Mr. Wentworth to agree to come to your apartment, Dr. Higgins? We could wire the place. Is there a room we could set up the equipment?"

"My office," Haley answered. "We could watch through the keyhole while we listen. There's a clear view of the kitchen. But I have to say, now that I'm thinking it through, I have a bad feeling about the whole idea. If Richard Wentworth is the nefarious Gerhardt Sommerfeld, Samantha would be in harm's way. There's got to be something else we could do without jeopardizing Samantha's safety."

Officer Bell was quick to agree. "You're right. We'll table this idea."

"Just hold on," Samantha said. "Don't I have a say? You'll be in the apartment with me, right? Both of you? That's three against one."

"She has a point," Tom said. "And I'll bring another officer with me, plus we'd be armed." His eyes glimmered with excitement. "Imagine if we brought this notorious spy down."

"Exactly," Samantha said. "And once I get him to confess, you can arrest him."

Haley scowled. "*If* you can get him to confess."

"I'll get him to confess," Samantha said bravely. "Just wait and see."

Samantha had barely settled into her desk the next morning when Mr. August beckoned her to see him in his office.

His request caused her to dry swallow. Was she going to get reprimanded for spending too much time out of the office? Should she tell him she was hot on a story about war spies? Would he believe her? Should she divulge it to him before she had something?

Samantha patted her hair and smoothed out her dress. With shoulders back she walked with as much dignity as she could muster, knowing that the eyes of the fellas in the room were watching her hips swing.

Let them look, and if Mr. August had a beef with her, she would make a stand. Her work on the ladies' pages had not suffered; in fact, she had to work twice as hard as Johnny and his ilk who only had to think about their next story.

"Mr. August?" Samantha said when she entered

the editor's office. Stacks of yesterday's newspapers lined the desktop, along with the usual coffee mug, ashtray, and cigar box. Immediately in front of him was a pile of unfolded letters.

"Miss Hawke, take a seat."

"Yes, sir." Samantha settled into an empty wooden chair. "Is there a problem, sir?"

"It depends on how you look at it." He stared at her over the rims of a new pair of glasses. "I ran your letter to the editor, anonymously, and as you predicted, it's caused a small dung storm."

Samantha inclined her head, waiting for more.

"We got more mail this morning than we have since the price for a dozen eggs went up to eighteen cents. Mostly from angry husbands telling us we got no business printing this dog do, but many from women thankful someone has the nerve to write about wife battery. One even calls it her 'secret shame behind closed doors.'"

Samantha still couldn't tell if Mr. August was pleased or upset. "So . . ."

Finally, a grin spread across his face. "We sold a lot of papers this morning, Miss Hawke."

"Oh, that's good, Mr. August."

"Nothing like a contentious debate to move papers. So, what I'm thinking is that you should write that piece, and we'll print it."

A ribbon of pleasure tied a bow in her stomach—not another letter to the editor but a *real* assignment.

"It'd be an opinion piece," Mr. August said, "but you might not want to use your real name." He tapped the pile of letters with a stubby finger. "Some of these gents are out for blood."

"What are you going to do with those letters, sir?" Samantha asked.

"Oh, we'll select the best ones to print."

He pushed the pile over to Samantha. "I've marked the ones I like. You can take them to Inky."

"Yes, sir, Mr. August."

Simeon "Inky" Isaacson managed the printing press. Samantha took the steps one floor down to the composing room and found him there.

"Well, hello there, Miss Hawke," Inky said. He was a wiry man with tobacco-stained teeth and inkstand fingers. "What can I do you for?"

"Mr. August would like these letters to the editor printed in tonight's paper."

Inky accepted the letters and took a cursory look. "Ah, the anon letter on wife beating." He shook his head and clucked his tongue. "Never understood how a man could treat his wife so badly. I believe women should be treated like treasures. I just wish my missus was still around."

Samantha put a hand to her heart. "Mr. Isaacson, that's so sweet."

"Yeah, well," he pointed his thumb over his shoulder at the men working behind him. "Don't let those horses know I got a soft side, eh? They'd get lazy."

Samantha couldn't wait to start on her assignment, but she had another errand she had to run first, one that made her pulse jump and her stomach drop. She had to find Mr. Wentworth and invite him to dinner.

Samantha, Haley, and Tom had decided the best move would be for Samantha to go to the Custom House and just to ask to see Wentworth and be forthright. Richard Wentworth, alias Gerhardt Sommerfeld, seemed like the kind of man who'd find such forwardness from a female tantalizing. At the time, Samantha had spoken with strong assurance about her ability to do such a brazen thing, but now her knees trembled.

"Mr. Wallace," she said as she approached the front desk. "I'd like to see Mr. Richard Wentworth."

"Do you have an appointment?"

It hadn't occurred to Samantha that she'd need to book an appointment.

"No, but he'll see me," she said boldly. "Tell him Miss Hawke is here."

"Right. The dame from the papers."

Samantha felt her lips tighten. "Yes. I'm a journalist."

As if quite certain his efforts would be wasted, Mr. Wallace rolled his eyes as he picked up the receiver. "Please connect me to Mr. Wentworth's office," he said. "Tell him a Miss Hawke," he covered the receiver and spoke to Samantha. "Paper?"

"The *Boston Daily Record.*"

"A Miss Hawke from the *Boston Daily Record* is here to see him. And no, she doesn't have an appointment."

The smug look dropped off the receptionist's face.

"Mr. Wentworth will see you. He's on the seventh floor."

The seventh floor? Samantha thought. *The same floor Mrs. Gray and Mr. Snow had fallen from to their deaths. How had she and Haley not known that*?

Samantha hesitated for a moment before getting into the elevator. *Was she about to take a nosedive from the seventh floor*? *No. Rick wouldn't be that bold—there were people around.*

The floor receptionist directed her to Rick's office, a nice corner office on the opposite side of the floor to Mrs. Gray's. *It could be possible that Rick Wentworth and Olivia Gray worked on the same floor for a time before running into each other. Oh, dear*, Samantha thought. *The shock that must have snapped when they caught sight of one another.*

Rick was waiting for her with his office door open. "This is a surprise, Miss Hawke." He waved her inside. "Take a seat."

"Actually, I'd rather stand. I won't take long."

"Oh, it sounds ominous."

Samantha giggled girlishly. "No, quite the opposite. I'm afraid I'm just nervous and about to do something scandalous."

Like Samantha knew he would, Rick smiled, and his eyes glinted with mischief.

"Do go on."

"My friend Dr. Higgins has gone away on a short trip, and she's asked me to look after her apartment. I wondered if you might like to join me for dinner tonight. At Dr. Higgins' home."

Rick's smile broadened, and he let out a soft chuckle. "Why, this is a surprise, Miss Hawke. Quite honestly, I didn't think you had it in you."

Oh, just wait, Samantha thought severely. Having applied an extra coat of mascara for the occasion, she batted her eyelashes. "Is that a yes?"

"Indeed, it is."

26

Samantha's bravado dissipated as the hands of the clock approached seven.

Rick. She called him that in her mind so she wouldn't mistakenly call him Sommerfeld. What a nightmare that would be!

Rick. Rick. Rick.

"Are you all right?" Haley asked. Her dark eyes showed the concern she had for her friend. "We can stop this if you're having second thoughts."

"No, I'm fine," Samantha said firmly. Succeeding at this would put a known criminal behind bars. And, she admitted, it would be a boost to her career. For a fleeting moment, she felt bad about keeping Johnny in the dark. Tom had insisted that they didn't involve him as this was a police matter. Having two civilians participating in the operation was already two too many.

Tom and a constable named Finch had installed microphones in the kitchen and living room. They'd set up the control station in Haley's office.

Molly had made a delicious meal of roasted chicken and potatoes, before leaving—somewhat reluctantly, she hated to miss out on the action—on an outing with Dr. Guthrie. Samantha chuckled inwardly. She'd never seen *that* romance coming. She thought they were adorable together but since Haley squirmed when Dr. Guthrie arrived to collect her housekeeper, Samantha guessed that Haley didn't feel the same way.

Tom left Haley's office and came into the kitchen. "We're ready," he said. His gaze locked with Samantha's, and she could read his concern for her there. But also, admiration and respect. She wasn't just another flighty, weak-natured female. *He's a good fellow. Maybe Haley is right. Maybe I should give him a chance.*

"Dr. Higgins, if you wouldn't mind sitting in Wentworth's place at the table, and Samantha—Miss Hawke—if you'd take your place, then please engage in conversation so we can test the recording."

Samantha and Haley did as Tom requested, and he disappeared behind Haley's closed office door. Earlier, Samantha and Haley had tested the keyhole. The kitchen table was in view, though there was no way to see the living room. Haley and Molly's bedrooms were down a hallway and of no use when it came to surveillance of the living areas.

Tom wanted them to speak in conversational tones, so Samantha turned to Haley. "Molly and Dr. Guthrie are a surprise. How did they meet?"

"Molly thought it would be nice if we invited my new boss for dinner, especially since he was a widower and new to the country. I don't think she had any thoughts beyond being hospitable. This growing . . . 'friendship' is a surprise to them as well."

"They're both immigrants from the United Kingdom, so they have that in common."

With an exaggerated British accent, Haley said, "Oh, quite!"

"You seem uncomfortable with it."

"Not with Molly seeing someone—I've encouraged her many times—it's just that he's my boss. Imagine if Bina and Mr. August started seeing each other."

Samantha nearly gagged at the thought. "I see what you mean."

Mr. Midnight hopped under the table where he threaded between their legs. Samantha, surprised at first, looked under the table and scooped him up. "Hello, Mr. Midnight," she said giving his head a nice pat. "Are you going to help me with our covert operation?"

Mr. Midnight let out a small meow in agreement as Samantha lowered him back to the floor.

Tom reappeared. "We picked that up loud and clear."

"Terrific," Haley said. "Please record over it. I wouldn't want Molly to overhear that conversation accidentally." She checked her watch. "Wentworth will be here any minute. We should take our places."

Tom braced Samantha's shoulders with his palms. "If you feel uncomfortable and want me to step in, just call for me."

The doorbell rang. Samantha's eyes flashed with both fear and determination.

Haley, along with Tom and Finch, quietly retreated to her office and closed the door.

Through the hidden microphones, Haley and Officer Bell could hear the front door unlock and Samantha's voice. "Hello, Rick."

"Samantha," Wentworth said warmly. "You look . . . amazing."

"These are lovely," Samantha said. "Thank you."

Haley couldn't see what he'd given her.

"The floral scent reminds me of you," Wentworth said, his words as smooth as a doll's cheek.

Ah, flowers, Haley thought.

Background rustling. *Wentworth removing his jacket?*

"Supper's ready if you'd like to follow me to the kitchen," Samantha said without a quiver or note of apprehension.

Proud of her friend, Haley grinned. It turned out that Samantha Hawke would've made a good spy herself, like Haley's London friend, Ginger.

"Let me just put these in a vase."

Now that they had entered the kitchen, Haley saw Samantha and Wentworth through the peephole. Samantha held a small bouquet of early pink roses.

"Now where would Dr. Higgins keep her vases?"

Haley mentally willed her to find them. *Far right cupboard, top shelf.*

Samantha proved to have good instincts and found one on her second try.

"I brought a little something to drink with dinner," Wentworth said. He opened the brown paper bag he'd been carrying and withdrew a clear glass bottle filled with a light golden liquid.

"Champagne?" Samantha said. "You wicked man!"

Tom Bell, with a scowl etched deeply on his face, nudged Haley aside. She reluctantly gave up her visual contact, but at least she could still hear loud and clear.

"You don't mind?" Wentworth continued. "Do

you? Most newsmen I know happily imbibe, despite the laws, but as a newswoman . . ."

Samantha's voice tinkled like a bell. "Don't be silly. I'd love a glass."

Haley could hear her searching the cupboards, probably looking for suitable glassware.

"Not flutes," Samantha said, "but these should do."

A loud gunshot-like sound caused Haley to flinch. She pushed Officer Bell aside.

Officer Bell whispered, "It's just the cork popping."

Haley bent low, lining her eyeball with the keyhole and saw Wentworth pour the champagne into the glasses and hand one to Samantha. *They're standing much too close*, Haley thought. *Arm's length*!

Samantha sipped politely, then said, "Please have a seat, Rick. Your place setting is on the opposite side of the table, if you don't mind. I like to be close to the stove."

Wentworth took his place like the conspirators had planned, his back to Haley's office door. She let go of the breath she'd been holding, now that Samantha was a safe distance away.

Officer Bell motioned for a turn at the keyhole. Frown lines etched his face and his hand rested on the handle of the gun in a holder on his hip. Haley took comfort at the sight of the weapon.

Now would be as good a time as any to grab my

gun from my purse and move it to the small of my back. The waistband on her loose, wide-leg pants was just tight enough to hold it in place. One sign of Samantha being in even the slightest bit of trouble, and she and Officer Bell, along with the quiet Constable Finch standing at the ready, would burst out of the office, guns blazing.

"Smells delicious," Wentworth said. Then he let out three consecutive sneezes. He promptly removed a handkerchief from his pants pocket.

"I'm dreadfully sorry about that," he said. "Is there a cat about?"

"Yes," Samantha said. "Are you allergic?"

"Only slightly," Wentworth said, returning the handkerchief. "The cat must've been in this room recently."

"He was. Do you want me to find him? I could put him out on the fire escape."

"No, no, no," Wentworth said, Haley thought a little too strongly. "It's fine. I don't want your lovely meal to get cold."

There was a moment of quiet as the meal commenced.

"This is unbelievably delicious," Wentworth said. "I hope you didn't go to too much expense. I know times are tough."

"Nonsense," Samantha said. "I'm a working girl."

"Yes, I read your piece on the waterfront crime you helped to solve. Must have been dangerous.

"Just me in the right place at the right time," Samantha said lightly. "Or me in the wrong place at the wrong time. I suppose it's how you look at it."

"I'm glad it had a happy ending for you that time."

That time?

Haley and Officer Bell exchanged a look. Was that a veiled threat?

"Let's toast, shall we," Wentworth added. "To us."

Officer Bell let out an audible growl, and Haley poked him. "Shh."

27

Samantha worked hard to keep from squirming underneath Wentworth's intense, shadowy blue-eyed gaze. She forced a smile as she took a small sip of her champagne, thankful that the nervousness she felt didn't manifest in her hands shaking. She took a bite of roasted carrot, and the burst of flavor momentarily distracted her. *How did Molly do it?*

Rick agreed as he let out a hum of approval.

"You are quite a cook, Samantha," he said. "I'd love to find out what other gifts you hide behind your professional journalist veneer."

Samantha ignored the innuendo. He was right about one thing, she was a professional journalist, and she had a job to do.

"I was born and raised in Boston," she said. "I know

a lot of people, but I've never run into you before the tragedy at the Custom House. How long have you lived here?"

"I'm new to the area. I'd had my fill of gray skies and damp weather in London, so I decided to give the warmer, tropical climes of Mexico a try."

Good, he admitted to being in Mexico, just as Johnny had stated.

"Mexico? That's a big change. Did you eventually grow bored with the incessant good weather? Sadly, besides a short trip to New York City, I've never been out of New England. Mexico seems so exotic, though I think I would miss the change of seasons."

"Eventually, yes. Surprisingly, I found I missed England. Boston is the closest representative of the old country in America, which is why I came. I was fortunate enough to land a job."

"It's quite miraculous, isn't it," Samantha said, "in this economy. Especially coming straight from Mexico."

"Yes, well, I happened to know someone who pulled strings." He raised his glass. "You'll admit that we're all where we are as a result of who we know."

Samantha hated to agree, but she too, had got her first job as a receptionist at the *Boston Daily Record* because she'd known the lady who'd worked there before her. Carla had left because she was getting married, and Samantha started working because her husband had disappeared.

"Were you still in England when the Great War broke out?"

Wentworth's head snapped up. "What?"

"I mean, you must've been, right? The king required all young men to enlist. Or is that why you fled to Mexico?" She tried to look innocent but wasn't sure if she was pulling it off. "Is that why you're staying in the USA and not going back?"

Wentworth's cheeks pulled up into a smile. "You're always on the job, aren't you, Miss Hawke? Is that why you invited me to dinner? Are you after a story?"

Samantha felt the heat of humiliation creep up her neck. She'd moved too fast! If she'd had more experience with this kind of thing, she would've eased in with her questions and had the skill to make it feel like a genuine conversation and not an interrogation.

She smiled flirtatiously. "I suppose I am, though I promise, it's not why I invited you. I'm trained to sniff out a good story or interest piece. It's my job, and how I make my living. Please forgive me."

"No harm done. I'll answer your questions because I like you, and if I can appease your curiosity, I'm happy to do it."

"Really, you don't—"

Wentworth raised a palm. "It's fine. I want to. I did serve in the war, but not as a soldier."

"Were you in a reserved occupation?"

"I'll be frank. I worked for the secret service."

Samantha's surprise was sincere. She'd hardly expected him to admit to covert activities, though he was trying to lead her to believe he'd worked for the British and not the Germans.

"Son of a gun!"

Wentworth grinned. "That always gets the ladies."

Samantha frowned. "Hey, are you saying it's not true?"

"Oh, it's true. But it's *secret*. So that's all I can tell you."

Drat! How on earth was she supposed to get him to confess to murder? Her gaze darted to the door of Haley's office. She wished she'd gotten more advice before they'd executed this plan. In a moment of vanity, she'd thought she could wrap Wentworth around her little finger with her feminine charm. Maybe she needed to pour it on more thickly.

Wentworth noticed her staring over his shoulder and turned to see what she was looking at. Impulsively, Samantha lifted the bottle of champagne.

"Rick, can I top you up?"

He refocused on her and lifted his glass. "Certainly. And what about you?" He frowned at her still-full glass. "You're not a fan of champagne? What do you like? I can get whatever you want. For next time."

If Samantha could succeed at this mission, there'd be no next time.

"A French red wine would be nice."

28

Haley's stomach clenched as she watched the pair through the keyhole. "I think we've underestimated him," she whispered. *How stupid of us to think Samantha could outwit a man who based his whole life on deceit*—a man with an intrinsic ability to make people believe in him and do his bidding. A seasoned two-faced man like that would spot falsehood a mile away.

"We have to abort."

Officer Bell disagreed. "Not yet. I think she can do it."

"And if she can't?"

Tom Bell patted his pistol. "I'm a good shot."

Samantha's voice reached them through the recording system. "I've heard the Germans had a pretty good secret service of their own."

"You're well versed on war maneuvers, Samantha."

"Well, I am a reporter. I have to know the news."

A chuckle from Wentworth. "Yes, the Germans were good. Very good."

Haley could hear the pride in the man's voice. His ego was so big he couldn't stop from boasting, even if it was cloaked in misdirection.

"Did you ever have personal dealings with them?" Samantha asked.

"Why don't we take this conversation to the living room where we'll be more comfortable. It's rather a long—"

"What happened?" Haley's heart skipped. "Why did it cut out?"

Constable Finch checked the machinery on Haley's desk. "Everything looks all right here."

"And we've lost eye contact," Haley said. Fear for Samantha's safety gripped her. "Oh my God! I think he's caught on. He could do anything to her, make her say anything."

Officer Bell nodded grimly. He reached for his gun, but before he could release it from its holder, the sound of the door pushing open stopped them.

"Tom!" Samantha's voice reached them, but not in time.

Haley's jaw dropped at the sight of Frieder Ginsberg's gun pointing right at her. There was no way she could reach for her pistol without him firing first.

"If you want the good doctor to live, Officer, you better drop your weapon." He waved his gun. "And tell the goon behind you to stay still. If he values his life, that is."

"How did you get in?" Haley asked. They hadn't heard the front door open or close, and the hinges had a very distinctive whine that Haley had failed to attend to.

"Fire escape, lady." Frieder Ginsberg made sounds of disapproval. "Even on the fourth floor, you should lock your windows."

Haley fumed. It was the middle of summer. No one locked their windows.

"Where's Miss Hawke?"

"Don't you worry. She's in safe hands."

Haley called out. "Samantha?"

They could barely hear her muffled reply, but it was enough to assure them she was still alive.

Haley took in her surroundings. Frieder Ginsberg was the only one with a gun in his hand, and there were three of them. If they could just distract him somehow and disarm him.

"Does your mother know you're here?"

Ginsberg's pale lashes fluttered and his scowl deepened. "My mother thinks I died a hero in the war. No one in this room's gonna tell her different."

"What are you doing in Boston? Why are you here in my home?"

"I know what you're trying to do, Dr. Higgins," Frieder Ginsberg said through tense lips. "This ain't my first walk around the block. I won't be distracted by you lot, now drop your weapons to the floor. All of you."

Haley, Officer Bell, and Constable Finch lowered their guns to the floor.

"Put your mitts on your heads."

"You know you've just provided proof of guilt, Mr. Ginsberg," Haley said.

The recording equipment on Haley's desk only elicited a grunt from their captor. "Those will be destroyed before any court will hear them."

Which meant the three in the room would be destroyed as well. And Samantha. These types didn't leave evidencc bchind.

"So, you admit to treason?"

"Treason is such a harsh word, Dr. Higgins. We merely helped our country how we could. No different from you."

"And now?"

"And now, we'll do what we have to do again. Your treaty crippled us, made it impossible to recover."

"Maybe you shouldn't have started the war in the first place," Officer Bell said.

"Maybe you should shut up!"

The beating of Haley's heart filled the deadly silence that fell on the room. She strained to hear Samantha and grew despairing when no sound between the reporter and Sommerfeld could be heard. She, Officer Bell, and Constable Finch were between a rock and a hard place. But even the best could be outmaneuvered.

Suddenly, a familiar head poked through the crack in the door. Haley's mind tried to make sense of it but failed. *Johnny Milwaukee*? What was he doing here?

"I trust you can take care of yourselves," Mr. Milwaukee said with his interminable grin. The office door closed quickly followed by the sound of a key in the lock.

Frieder Ginsberg protested, "Hey!"

During the German's attempt to open the door, both Haley and Officer Bell went for their guns. Haley got off the first shot.

29

Samantha knew she was in trouble the moment Wentworth suggested they move to the living room; however, she couldn't think of a sane reason to deny his request. She picked up their two glasses by the stems with one hand, and the bottle with the other. It could perhaps inspire him to drink and perhaps loosen his lips. Her intention, once she delivered her items to the coffee table, was to claim the armchair sitting at an angle toward the couch, but Wentworth had other plans. He grabbed her wrist.

"Come, sit with me."

His hold verged on uncomfortable, not tight enough to cause pain, but strong enough that she would be forced to create a scene if she tried to pull free.

"Have you ever been married, Rick?" she asked, hoping to throw him off.

He lowered himself to the couch forcing her to do the same, leaving only inches between them.

"Yes, but I suspect that you already knew that. Just as I know that you have as well. You're not the only one who checks up on their dates."

Samantha swallowed back the fear she felt. "I was married for less than a year before my husband left me."

"I can't imagine any man wanting to leave such a lovely woman as you."

"Well, I'm not sure he did it intentionally. I think he got in with a bad crowd." This was an assumption Samantha had only recently considered now that she'd had personal experience with the criminal underbelly of Boston. "I think he's dead."

"My wife is dead too."

Samantha's heart thudded in her chest. "I'm sorry. Not recently, I hope."

Wentworth grinned.

"I love the game you're playing, Samantha." He chuckled. "I knew you had spunk, when I saw you with those other journalists. And you're attractive too. I knew I could gain your interest, convince you to go out with me. I needed to know what you knew, or rather, what you might find out."

"That's rather bold and conceited of you," Samantha said indignantly.

"It was, wasn't it, Mrs. Rosenbaum." There was a deadness in his eyes when he smiled, and Samantha couldn't believe she'd ever found him attractive.

"Rosenbaum. That's Jewish, isn't it? I can't imagine what drove you to marry a Jew. Unless you weren't a good girl. . ."

"Mr. Wentworth, that is enough!"

"We're back to formal names, are we? That's fine. I think we both know we've crossed a line and we can't go back."

Samantha stood with real indignation, only to be forcibly returned to her seat by a hard tug on the arm.

"Not so fast, my Jewish friend."

"I'll have you know I'm not Jewish. Not that it matters."

"You have a Jewish daughter and mother-in-law. That's guilt by association."

Samantha was astounded. Sure, anti-Semitism was alive and well in Boston, but it was the first time she'd experienced it firsthand.

"I think it's time you left, Mr. Wentworth."

Wentworth shook his head and clucked his tongue. "First, you tell me everything you know, and then I'll let you go."

Samantha couldn't help but cast a glance at the

wire in the room. It had been carefully hidden behind the Areca palm but was now pulled loose and with two ends dangling. Her heart jumped to her throat. It had been *cut*. How had that happened? Wentworth had been in her sight the whole time.

"All I know is you have ties to Germany, and you were once married to Olivia Gray. Did you kill her? Did you kill your ex-wife and her colleague, Mr. Snow?"

"See, this is the problem with being too smart, love."

"Why? Why did you do it?"

Wentworth snorted. "I'm in America in service to my country."

"Germany."

"Yes, love. Germany. Olivia and I had only been married a year. Unfortunately for both of us, I was German and no longer welcome in England. I left to go back to Germany, and she was going to join me there, when the war was over. But, by the time the war ended, I was a changed man, dedicated to the cause of the Fatherland. It was decided that I could be of better use to my country without the complication of a British wife. She was told that I'd died in battle.

"Quite honestly, I lost track of her. I really thought she was living in some God-forsaken English village."

"And then?"

"And then, much to my surprise and hers, we bumped into each other in the hall at the Custom House. I tried to make her believe I only looked like her dead husband, but she was too astute for that. It was an impulsive move, on my part. Finding her alone in her office, I pulled the fire alarm, then tossed her out the window. She put up a bit of a fight, I'll give her that."

"You heartless son—"

In an instant, Wentworth had his arm around Samantha's throat. She grabbed at his arm and felt his skin snag under her nails. Having no self-defense training, she was the sheep at the slaughter. She would die at the hands of this madman, and he'd probably escape justice once again. Her vision blurred, and she feared she was seeing things. Beyond Wentworth's shoulder, she thought she'd seen Johnny Milwaukee in the room.

Suddenly, Mr. Midnight was on the couch, traipsing over their legs, the pricking of his sharp claws piercing the skin.

"Ouch!" Wentworth slapped at the cat.

Mr. Midnight hissed before hopping off.

Wentworth broke into a fit of sneezing.

Samantha took advantage of this turn of fortune an added a sharp hit to Wentworth stomach with her elbow.

He released a loud *ooff* as she sprinted away.

Johnny turned out to be as real as rain. He attacked

Wentworth, knocking over the armchair. Mr. Midnight screeched and ran for cover. Johnny appeared to have the upper hand, but then in an instant, Wentworth was on top, releasing blows to Johnny's face. Samantha sprung to action and grabbed an unlit oil lamp. She brought it down on Wentworth's head, stepped back and gasped.

Wentworth stilled, then fell to one side. Johnny scrambled out from underneath him, one hand cupping his chin.

"Oh my, did I kill him?"

"No, doll, he's breathing. But good on you, though I was just waiting for him to tire out. I had the next move all lined up."

Samantha rolled her eyes.

Johnny removed his tie and bound Wentworth's hands behind his back. When he searched for something to bind Wentworth's feet, Samantha slipped off her narrow belt.

"Use this."

Wentworth moaned as his eyes flickered open. His gaze landed on Samantha. Through dry lips he said, "you hit me", then he passed out again.

Finally, Samantha had a chance to ask the question begging to be answered. "What are you doing here?"

"I'm hot on a story, Sam," Johnny said, his palm cupping his jaw. "And this was where the story led me.

I've been tailing Ginsberg and Sommerfeld a while, and when I saw you on a date with—"

"It wasn't a date! I was on the job."

"Fine. I didn't know what story you were after—"

"So you deliberately baited me with the names?"

"All's fair in love and war, doll. You wanted to catch a murderer and I, a man guilty of war crimes. Just so happened we wanted the same guy."

"Well, that's good fortune for both of us then," she said snidely. "But how did you end up here? Tonight?"

"I was following Ginsberg. Imagine my surprise when he led me up the good doctor's fire escape, and then seeing you. . ."

Samantha nodded in understanding, then pointed to Wentworth. "Do you think he's secure enough?"

"Hmm," Johnny said, with a cocky grin, but before he could get his next quip off, they heard a gunshot down the hall.

Frieder Ginsberg writhed on the floor and screamed about his leg.

"Find something to tie off the blood flow," Haley instructed as she stepped around the wounded man. Her only concern at the moment was for Samantha. Johnny Milwaukee was in the apartment somewhere too, and possibly in danger.

Haley used the office door key she had in her pocket to unlock the door, thankful that whatever skeleton key Johnny had used hadn't been left in the keyhole. She brandished her gun and stepped stealthily down the hall. Feeling like a cop in one of those Hollywood gangster movies, she stormed into the living room ready to fire.

"Haley, are you all right?" Samantha asked.

Samantha's voice reassured her as she took in the room. Tied to a chair, Sommerfeld sat with his hands bound behind his back, his head slack.

"We heard a shot," Johnny said. He nodded toward the gun that Haley still held at the ready.

"Yes," Haley lowered her weapon. "Mr. Ginsberg's been wounded."

"May I?" Johnny said. He held out a palm. "I just don't want Mr. Sunshine over there to get any ideas."

Haley gave her gun to Johnny then went to Samantha's side. "Are you okay? You had me scared for a minute."

Samantha started shaking. "Now, that it's over, I think it's finally setting in."

Officer Bell stormed into the room. "Everything okay in here?" He eyed Sommerfeld tied to a chair with his head slowly rising and emitted a groan. He quickly added handcuffs to Sommerfeld's restraints, then went directly to Samantha. "You were very brave. Very, very brave. I'm sorry we put you through that."

"It's fine, Tom. I'm fine. I'm glad we stopped him."

Tom's gaze and concern were palpable, and Haley hoped he'd remain professional and not impulsively pull Samantha into an embrace.

Mr. Milwaukee had the same concern as he loudly cleared his throat. "Officer Bell," he said. "Please arrest this man."

Haley put an arm around Samantha's shoulder and pulled her aside. "Tell me what happened."

Samantha's gaze darted to Sommerfeld who was now awake enough to glare back. "He had his arm around my neck."

"And Johnny rescued you?"

"No, actually, it was Mr. Midnight."

Samantha relayed the story, and Haley couldn't help but grin a little.

30

Samantha stood in front of Johnny Milwaukee as if they were a couple about to waltz.

But they weren't about to dance.

"What you gotta do, doll, is put your fists up in front of your face, see." Johnny lifted his closed palms, the right one above the other, close to his neck and jaw, his bruising still apparent. "You wanna protect your neck. And if a guy goes for you, you stick your arm up like this to block him. Then give a good whack in the gut, right here under the ribcage with your other hand." With snakebite quickness, he did the moves.

"I know most dames want to go for the *cajones*," he continued, "but believe me, that's all we men are thinking about protectin'. A strike to the gullet and you'll have a grown man gasping for breath. Now you try it." Then he added with a grin, "Just, ya know, don't hurt me."

Samantha's inability to defend herself against Wentworth-Sommerfeld had scared her enough to let Johnny become her teacher.

Again.

Everything Samantha knew about the newspaper business she'd learned by watching the other reporters, and most often, Johnny. He was the kind of guy she loved to hate.

And hated to love.

Johnny snapped his fingers in front of her face. "Dollface. If you're gonna beat your attacker, you can't just check out like that."

"I didn't check out. I'm just reviewing what you said before I try it." Then she punched him in the gut.

"Oof! Dang it, Sam. I wasn't ready."

"You said never to let your guard down, Johnny."

She played it tough, but inwardly she'd never meant to do him harm. "Are you okay?"

She laid an arm on his shoulder. In an instant, Johnny had her in an arm hold, much like Sommerfeld had done.

"Don't ever let your guard down, Sam."

"I can't—"

Johnny loosened his hold. "You got a split second to get out of a hold like this, doll. No time to waste, do you hear? Shrug your shoulders as hard as you can—before I tighten. Otherwise, it's too late, and you're dead. Shrug!"

Samantha shrugged hard, and amazingly, Johnny could not tighten the hold like before.

"Now don't waste your time grabbing my arm. You're not gonna be able to shake me loose."

"What do I do, then?"

"Take a small step to the right."

Samantha did so.

"See what you did there? You opened me up for attack. Use your elbow to hit me in the gut, here, right below my ribs. Just like you did on Wentworth. Easy now, just go through the motions."

Samantha made a fist then pulled her elbow back until it touched Johnny's stomach.

"Now use that fist and swing it down like a hammer."

"At your, uh, cajones?"

"Yeah." Johnny let her go. "But try that move at home, hey. With a pillow or somethin'."

She grinned.

"And for good measure, you can stomp on the top of the fellow's foot. It's bony there and, let me tell ya, it hurts."

Samantha raised a brow. "Someone had reason to stomp on your foot, Johnny?"

"Maybe it was accidental. But it got the point across all the same."

Samantha eyed her faux opponent. "Where d'you learn this?"

"There now, I can't tell you all my secrets. And as much as I'd like to stay here and get, uh, more acquainted, I've gotta run." He set his fedora back on his head and tipped it in her direction. "See ya later, Sam."

"But, do I lock up or something?" Johnny's friend had opened the gym up for him as a favor.

"If you don't mind."

By the time Samantha got home, she'd decided. She was going to have Seth officially declared dead. She told herself that Johnny Milwaukee had nothing to do with it.

He didn't.

Not really.

Bina didn't take the news well.

Samantha had expected a tirade and even the need to duck a pot as it sailed across the room. She hadn't expected tears.

Bina slumped onto the wooden chair, the one with a short leg, and rocked slightly. She put her face into her hands and sobbed.

"Oh, Bina!"

Samantha didn't know what to do. Not once since

she'd known Bina Rosenbaum had the woman shed one tear. Not even when Talia was born. Samantha surprised herself with her sudden compassion for Bina.

"Deep down, you must know it's true. I'm so sorry, Bina. I wish I were wrong."

Bina looked up with bloodshot eyes. "If you were wrong, Seth would be home. My boy wouldn't shrug his responsibilities."

Samantha awkwardly rubbed her mother-in-law's shoulders as the woman blew her nose into a handkerchief. "I know."

"He might leave you," Bina continued, "but he wouldn't leave his daughter and his mother."

There, the old Bina was back.

But she had a point, Samantha thought. Seth had to be dead. It was time to declare it—time to take back her life.

Even after the arrests had been made, their tipster never came forward, but Haley had a hunch. Another trip to the Custom House confirmed her suspicions, and when pressed, the mail clerk, Miss Sheila Everson, admitted it was her.

"Please don't tell anyone, Dr. Higgins," she said. Tears spouted from glassy eyes, and her thick glasses made them look large. "I'm just so embarrassed. Mr.

Wentworth was so charming, and I don't get a lot of attention, you know, but then, well, he was a brute! After that, I kept my distance as much as possible, circling backward if necessary, ducking behind corners and file cabinets, just to avoid him. That's why he didn't see me. I saw him push Mrs. Gray out the window!

"I know I should've gone to the police right away, but I was afraid I'd be the next one to die. If only I had, Mr. Snow might still be alive."

Along with various war crimes, Sommerfeld had confessed to killing Olivia Gray and Philip Snow. He was arrogant enough to think the police would eventually conclude it had been a murder-suicide on Snow's part: he killed her because she broke up with him, and then he jumped out of guilt.

Haley did her best to comfort the poor woman.

"What Mr. Wentworth did to Mrs. Gray and Mr. Snow is not your fault. The responsibility lies strictly with Mr. Wentworth."

"Thank you, Dr. Higgins." Miss Everson lifted her glasses and dabbed her eyes. "I need to get back to work now."

"Of course. Miss Everson?"

"Yes?"

"Keep your chin up."

. . .

When Haley got home later that day, Molly fluttered like a butterfly as she prepared for another dinner date with Dr. Guthrie. "Don't you think dining out is an unnecessary extravagance? I feel like I'm rubbing my good fortune in the faces of those who struggle so much."

"Just think about the people you're helping by eating out," Haley said. "The restaurant owner, the chef, the waiters, the dishwasher. I'm sure they all appreciate you being extravagant once in a while.

"Well, when you put it that way." Molly wore a blue high-waisted pleated dress with a cute little shawl and a short-brimmed straw hat. She turned in front of Haley like a fashion model. "How do I look?"

"You look amazing, Molly," Haley said sincerely. "Dr. Guthrie is sure to approve."

"And you're sure . . . you don't mind?"

Haley knew what Molly was referring to. She and Molly had never discussed how Haley felt about the burgeoning relationship between Molly and Haley's boss, but Molly was intuitive. Haley hadn't hidden that she wasn't overly excited about the pairing. On the one hand, she was worried about Molly's feelings should Dr. Guthrie ever change his tune, and on the other, she couldn't imagine Molly ever moving out. *I've gotten used to her company, not to mention her cooking, but*

I'm jumping the queue as they say in England. Dr. Guthrie isn't about to pop the question.

"I don't mind," Haley said. "I'm glad you make each other happy."

The knock on the door announced Dr. Guthrie's arrival, and Haley had to give him credit for climbing all those stairs to get there. He wasn't exactly a young chicken.

Haley smiled at Molly. "Go have fun."

"You too," Molly said, referring to Haley's forthcoming outing with Dr. Mitchell. Haley never referred to their times spent together as dates. That would conclude that there was something romantic between them and there wasn't. He had tickets for the opera and had invited her to join him. It was something he often did, and whenever she could, she agreed.

Haley disappeared into her office to give Molly and Dr. Guthrie privacy. She opened her desk drawer and pulled out a green three-ring binder. Written in bold letters on the front was *MURDER INVESTIGATION OF JOSEPH HIGGINS*.

Inside were all the notes and newspaper clippings related to Joe's death, along with the pictures the police had taken of the crime scene. She'd lost count of how often she'd read through these notes and studied the pictures. Despite this, she knew a piece of the puzzle was missing.

She closed the binder and slipped it back into the drawer.

"I haven't forgotten about you, Joe."

Haley checked the time and realized she needed to hurry if she planned to be ready to meet Gerald on time. Her bedroom was plain but tidy with matching bedroom furniture that Molly kept dust free. There was a quilt on the bed with matching pillow shams and curled up in a black furry ball at the foot of it was Mr. Midnight.

Haley pressed her face into his soft belly as she scrubbed his ears. "Hey, hero." She'd been calling him that since Gerhardt Sommerfeld's arrest after learning the role her cat had played in Samantha's rescue. When Molly had heard, she'd given Mr. Midnight a whole piece of chicken as a reward.

Haley chose a simple black floor-length dress and added a shiny green belt for accent. She wasn't one for wearing makeup, but she made an exception for the opera. She applied smoky eye shadow and red lipstick and even plucked a few eyebrow hairs to form the arch Samantha had written about in her articles.

Yes, Haley now read the ladies' pages and was surprised to find she enjoyed them.

A knock at the door had her quickly checking her wristwatch. She still had some time. Had Gerald decided to pick her up after all?

"I thought I was meeting—"

Haley left the sentence dangling at the sight of the man on the other side of the door. It wasn't Gerald Mitchell.

"Jack?"

Officer Jack Thompson, her onetime brief but intense flame, stood across the threshold.

His eyes sparkled as he took her in.

"I hope I'm not interrupting."

If you enjoyed reading *Death on the Tower.* please help others enjoy it too.

Recommend it: Help others find the book by recommending it to friends, readers' groups, discussion boards and by suggesting it to your local library.

Suggest it to your local librarian.

Review it: Please tell other readers why you liked this

book by reviewing it on Amazon or Goodreads.

** Please do not use spoilers in your review**

DEATH ON HANOVER
A Higgins & Hawke Mystery # 3

Death by design. . .

Investigative reporter Sam Hawke, alias Mrs. Samantha Rosenbaum, is the first on the scene—what luck!—when a body is found in the yard of St. Stephen's Church on Hanover Street in Boston.

Dr. Haley Higgins, the assistant Chief Medical Examiner finds the modus operandi of the crime eerily familiar to that of her brother's, an unsolved murder that has plagued her for years.

Set in the 1930s, this third book in the Higgins & Hawke mystery series will have you biting your nails as Haley and Samantha's pasts collide. Will Haley finally get to the bottom of the mystery behind brother's death? Will their friendship survive the truth?

Buy on AMAZON or read for FREE on Kindle Unlimited.

Read on for an excerpt.

For information on the next new releases and deals, be sure to sign up for Lee's newsletter!

MURDER on the SS Rosa is where we first meet Haley Higgins. If you haven't started the Ginger Gold Mystery series, now's your chance!

Murder's a pain in the bow!

It's 1923 and bright young thing Ginger Gold makes a cross-Atlantic journey from Boston to London, England. When the ship's captain is found dead in a most intriguing fashion, Ginger is only too happy to lend her assistance to the handsome Chief Inspector Basil Reed.

This fun, jazz-age whodunit has readers saying

"Lady Gold is a charming heroine" and "can't stop reading!"

Murder on the SS Rosa will have you laughing, crying, and guessing until the last page.

Get started and download the first book in this binge-worthy series today.

Read on AMAZON
or read it for Free on Kindle Unlimited

ABOUT THE AUTHOR

Lee Strauss is a USA TODAY bestselling author of The Ginger Gold Mysteries series, The Higgins & Hawke Mystery series, The Rosa Reed Mystery series (cozy historical mysteries), A Nursery Rhyme Mystery series (mystery suspense), The Perception series (young adult dystopian), The Light & Love series (sweet romance), The Clockwise Collection (YA time travel romance), and young adult historical fiction with over a million books read. She has titles published in German, Spanish and Korean, and a growing audio library.

When Lee's not writing or reading she likes to cycle, hike, and stare at the ocean. She loves to drink caffè lattes and red wines in exotic places, and eat dark chocolate anywhere.

For more info on books by Lee Strauss and her social media links, visit leestraussbooks.com. To make sure you don't miss the next new release, be sure to sign up for her newsletter!

Discuss the books, ask questions, share your opinions.

Fun giveaways! Join the Lee Strauss Readers' Group on Facebook for more info.

Love vintage pins? Follow me on Pinterest!

Did you know you can follow your favourite authors on Bookbub? If you subscribe to Bookbub — (and if you don't, why don't you? - They'll send you daily emails alerting you to sales and new releases on just the kind of books you like to read!) — follow me to make sure you don't miss the next Ginger Gold Mystery!

www.leestraussbooks.com
leestraussbooks@gmail.com

MORE FROM LEE STRAUSS

On AMAZON

HIGGINS & HAWKE MYSTERY SERIES (cozy 1930s historical)

The 1930s meets Rizzoli & Isles in this friendship depression era cozy mystery series.

Death at the Tavern

Death on the Tower

Death on Hanover

GINGER GOLD MYSTERY SERIES (cozy 1920s historical)

Cozy. Charming. Filled with Bright Young Things. This Jazz Age murder mystery will entertain and delight you with its 1920s flair and pizzazz!

Murder on the SS Rosa

Murder at Hartigan House

Murder at Bray Manor

Murder at Feathers & Flair

Murder at the Mortuary

Murder at Kensington Gardens

Murder at St. George's Church

The Wedding of Ginger & Basil

Murder Aboard the Flying Scotsman

Murder at the Boat Club

Murder on Eaton Square

Murder by Plum Pudding

Murder on Fleet Street

Murder at Brighton Beach

Murder in Hyde Park

Murder at the Royal Albert Hall

Murder in Belgravia

THE ROSA REED MYSTERIES

(1950s cozy historical)

Murder at High Tide

Murder on the Boardwalk

Murder at the Bomb Shelter

Murder on Location

Murder and Rock 'n' Roll

Murder at the Races

Murder at the Dude Ranch

Murder in London

LADY GOLD INVESTIGATES (Ginger Gold companion short stories)

Volume 1

Volume 2

Volume 3

Volume 4

A NURSERY RHYME MYSTERY SERIES(mystery/sci fi)

Marlow finds himself teamed up with intelligent and savvy Sage Farrell, a girl so far out of his league he feels blinded in her presence - literally - damned glasses! Together they work to find the identity of @gingerbreadman. Can they stop the killer before he strikes again?

Gingerbread Man

Life Is but a Dream

Hickory Dickory Dock

Twinkle Little Star

THE PERCEPTION TRILOGY (YA dystopian mystery)

Zoe Vanderveen is a GAP—a genetically altered person. She lives in the security of a walled city on prime water-front property alongside other equally beautiful people with extended life spans. Her brother Liam is missing. Noah Brody, a boy on the outside, is the only one who can help ~ but can she trust him?

Perception

Volition

Contrition

LIGHT & LOVE (sweet romance)

Set in the dazzling charm of Europe, follow Katja, Gabriella, Eva, Anna and Belle as they find strength, hope and love.

Sing me a Love Song

Your Love is Sweet

In Light of Us

Lying in Starlight

PLAYING WITH MATCHES (WW2 history/romance)

A sobering but hopeful journey about how one young German boy copes with the war and propaganda. Based on true events.

A Piece of Blue String (companion short story)

THE CLOCKWISE COLLECTION (YA time travel romance)

Casey Donovan has issues: hair, height and uncontrollable trips to the 19th century! And now this ~ she's accidentally taken Nate Mackenzie, the cutest boy in the school, back in time. Awkward.

Clockwise

Clockwiser

Like Clockwork

Counter Clockwise

Clockwork Crazy

Clocked (companion novella)

Standalones

Seaweed

Love, Tink

ACKNOWLEDGMENTS

Like the old adage, "It takes a village to raise a child," it takes a village to publish a book. With a full heart of gratitude I'd like to thank my "village."

Angelika Offenwanger - developmental editor, who reads the first dreadful drafts and helps me keep the story from falling off the rails. She's also a friend. (Thanks for your support!)

Robbie Bryant - line editor, who cleans up the first "finished" draft.

Heather Belleguelle - beta reader extraordinaire, who helps me to polish the story and complete the wordsmithing. (The day you quit is the day I quit. 😁)

Shadi Bleiken - administrator and social media guru, who helps me keep all the strings tied together and get the word out. She's a gift to La Plume Press and to the Strauss family!

Norm Strauss - partner in life and in crime. I love how we can work and play together and never stop finding something to laugh about.

Made in the USA
Middletown, DE
10 October 2021

49988466R00151